BLOOD ROSE CASTLE OF DOOM

A FANTASY NOVEL

JONATHAN EVAN HUDSON

BLOOD ROSE CASTLE OF DOOM

PROLOGUE
GRUNDER

Grunder of the Tuskerville Clan took a deep, slow breath of the chilly dry air of Dirlop Mountain, and did his best not to gasp, yank any bit of his waist-long beard, or even hurrumpf at the sight in the far, far, blue distance.

That sight … it couldn't be.

But off in the far, far blue distance, on top of that blistering high and craggy lone mountain known as Razorspine Peak, there was now a looming high and massive castle. A castle of blood red and dark gray stone. It appeared overnight, somehow, and its many sheer sleek battlements, zigzagging towers and twisting keeps all defied gravity itself, never mind the gatehouses that floated around it … and not on the solid reliable ground!

Crazy … like out of some drunken elf's tale … but for his

whole hundred and twenty years, Razorspine Peak was a lone barren mountain full of rocks so razor sharp, nothing in all of Altaarith continent could hope to climb it.

Yet all together, that castle looked like some a massive red and gray rose of sinister ... orc menace ... no.

Orcs were practically human warthogs. Beasts with some form of man, and the demented mind of the beast they looked like. They couldn't hope to build something that spectacular. Even dwarfs would ... struggle. Forget elves. They were like extra scrawny humans with dagger pointy ears jutting out the sides of their head, and stunk of fruit and ugh. Don't think of those elves this early in the morning.

Humans ... no. They were still well behind dwarves in technology.

None of the lightling or darklings races could manage it.

Grunter did grunt. Finally. Fiddle with his skullcap of reliable dark dwarven steel. The ale from last night still lingered in his throat, but his dinner of lamb stew should keep the liquor from affecting his brain but no, even without a solid meal today, and todays few sips of morning ale to get a dwarf going right, a dwarf had to trust his eyes, since who else could he trust as much than his own eyesight?

Grunter stood up from the flat reliable seat of stone he had fallen asleep on ... and spat to the side.

Bing. Onto the dusty rocky ground.

Then he looked at the sinister castle against but ... it was gone?

Impossible ... could there be something in the air ... a

scentless toxin that could make a dwarf less sound in the head.

But these craggy rocks and towering high boulders, they were familiar. Plenty of times he had woken up here after much needed R&R after a rambunctious night with overtalkive dwarven women. Don't get him wrong, dwarf women were the best of the best, especially the stoutest ones. Meaty and just the right kind of soft cozy beards down beyond their wide, wide waists, but sometimes a dwarf needed some time alone, and this spot on Dirlop Mountain, great for some alone time, and one of the best in all of the Altaarith Continent, in his opinion.

There was no chance there was bad air here. The wind was chilling the place, but kept it fresh. Fresh, crisp morning mountain air. Nothing to fear. Nothing to cause strange … visions.

At a time like this … a mate would of been nice. Someone to confide in, but no.

Regrets were for fools.

He'd find his mate in time. Help continue his clan's blood line but … no. He was fifty years too young for a wife. He still had another hundred or so years before dwarf women would start looking at younger dwarfs.

Plenty of time left.

Grunter was on an abandoned offshoot of the main stone road. The main stone road was wide enough for several wagons going in either direction and it wound hundreds of feet slow and steadily up into the dwarven town of Dirlop, the town which was, of course, chiseled inside Dirlop Mountain. All the roads on this wonderfully craggy mountain were chiseled carefully, smooth and reliable. They never worn down. No potholes. No cracks.

Nothing like unreliable human and elven roads.

Not to mention the disaster that were orc roads.

That most of the sky to his other side was still the bright glowing orange of sunrise … the main gatehouse should be open by the time he returned. No doubt he'd be assigned to scout that castle out.

So with an eyescope handy, and no Tuskerville dwarf would go without his trusty eyescope. It was a hand sized cylinder of the blackest of black iron alloy, the kind forged only by the best dwarfs. The lens was carefully crafted by the finest Tuskerville techniques so secret that even he hadn't been taught them … yet. Maybe once he was old enough to settle down with a wife, and finish his scouting days for good.

A whiles away, then. If only most of his Tuskerville Clan hadn't been summoned to the north to deal with a rowdy bunch of troublemakers that … hurrumpf, and hurrumpf was right, leaving him behind, but someone had to watch out for Dirlop.

And what he saw through the eyescope … he finally did gasp. The mountain known as Razorspine Peak … there were still signs of that sinister castle being there. It just … wasn't visible to the naked eye, not from here. His hackles shot sky high and then some.

The mayor needed to know right – ack!

His chest … something … an arrow? The shaft was as black as the abyss and vulture feathered and … an orc arrow?!

A laugh behind him. A girlie cackle. From a scrawny twig kind of a witch. And the stink of overgroomed beast.

"Zee lookout is finished, no? Just like Dirlop."

Grunter growled. "Why you ..."

He spun, lunging, but a sudden chill. And he knew no more.

CHAPTER 1
JAKON

Taking another slow deeeep breath of the sweltering hot and dry air, Jakon Dawdora did his best not to gasp, scratch his beard (as short and stubby as his black beard was), or even give his best dwarven hurrumpf at the sight in that far, far and all too blue distance.

Nope.

But on that towering high and amazingly craggy mountain known as Razorspine Peak ... it couldn't be ... but ...

A massive castle.

Like the mountain was just a thick stone stem and the castle a massive huge rose. A blood-red rose blighted with blotches of black. There were even sleek and spiny gatehouses around it. Like the gatehouses were thorns and the stairways were tendrils.

It just ... couldn't be. The castle wasn't there yesterday.

Just the mountain was there yesterday. An unexplored

mountain. The rocks were too razor sharp to travel up it, but Jakon would find a way. One day, when he was allowed a closer look. Eventually. When he was allowed to leave Dirlop on his own.

One day.

His bedroom window was round and wide despite the wall being sleek gray stone, so he could easily see the thick craggy forest of pine and oaks below. From here the forest was like a carpet along the vast valley full of moors and cliffs. It only hinted at the vast distance between Dirlop and Razor-spine Peak.

Yet still ... this sweltering heat meant his dad and his apprentices were already working hard in the family smithery since before sunrise, so they probably missed this sight, and ... ha!

Jakon barked a laugh so hard he could taste last night's dinner of mutton stew. He grinned so wide, he stroked his stubble once again. He was twenty and yet only had stubble. Not a true dwarf's beard, but no matter. It was finally growing in. Finally.

And now this castle ...

His eyes, he couldn't stop them. They glanced to the side, at his bookshelf, chiseled into the sleek gray wall. Five shelves and each shelf was modeled after the gears Jakon used to love forging in his dad's smithy, until his human half kicked in and sigh. Dwarven smithery techniques were too different from human smith techniques, too incompatible with humans, so ... sigh.

Being half-human, half-dwarf ...not always a blessing but ... like any dwarf would say, regrets are for fools and elves.

Just make tomorrow count even more!

Or in his case, today!

Still, Jakon tried to glance over at the four upper shelves packed full of leatherbacks more befitting of a well-read dwarf. Books about minerals and rocks. About histories and clans. Explorations and wars against orcs and worse, but no.

His eyes were glued once again to the bottom shelf, the shelf his mom, his human mom insisted his dad let him have. It grabbed his eyes and never let go since he started collecting and reading them ten years ago, when his human side ended his future as a dwarven smith forever. That very shelf was full of cheap flimsy paperbacks known as dime dreadfuls, but the stories in them ... so wild and crazy, yet only the most drunken dwarf could manage to tell them so well.

And one dime dreadful in particular ... called the *Blood Rose of Doom*.

Face out, because he hadn't had the chance to start it yet, but right on the cover, the exact same castle!

What were the chances ... that ... wha ... where did the castle go?!

It couldn't be ... but ... a dwarf trusted his eyes.

He saw what he saw.

Jakon threw on dark blue jerkin and navy slacks, and with his thick leather boot thunking the stone floor, he headed out proudly and eager for a hearty dwarven breakfast.

Ready to spread the news far and wide.

CHAPTER 2
JAKON

Yet that smell ... strawberries and cream? Jakon took another deep breath.

Yeah. Strange, dessert for breakfast?

And ... it was ... sniff, sniff, ah! Toppled with a liquid spice. That secret clear but shiny spice mom always used on the strawberries to give them the perfect sweet crisp twang. A secret spice she never had much of, and so she always saved it for special occasions.

Always.

So the question was ... what's the special occasion? No birthdays. No holidays.

Maybe a special visitor then? Without telling him? Strange. No. Probably not.

This hallway was straight like a hammer handle should be, but wide enough for the stoutest dwarf. Paintings chiseled into the wall showed his dad's side of the family, the

Dawdora Clan. All stout dwarfs, all with long braided beards down to the floor, both men and women, and all beaming proud of their dwarven lineage. They all seemed to look down at him as he marched down this hallway. But ever since his human side took over, it made Jakon into a lean and mean kind of guy, rather than thick and stout and truly bearded … sigh, even dwarf women by his age had better beards.

He might as well be marching down an aisle of judgment. Judged unworthy.

But a dwarf was a dwarf. Half or not.

And Jakon was still a Dawdora. He kept his back straight and high. Not a hint of slouching. Worrying about judgement like that, only elves worried about that nonsense. He'd just find another way other than smithing to prove himself a true dwarf.

Dwarves took on challenges head on. And each day, another challenge to face head on.

His nose proved as true as his eyes, but as a dwarf, that wasn't a surprise. It was expected.

A dwarf's nose was amazing, half human or not.

The kitchen was at the end of the hallway, and it was like the anvil to the hammer. The room was even shaped like an anvil, with sleek gray walls curved just right and diamonds sheening bright. All to remind everyone here of the importance of smithery, especially to this family's bloodline. In the center there was a small round table of the blackest of black iron. It was molded to look like concentric solid rings of black roses. It was a wedding gift to his mom, from his dad.

Three chairs of the same rosy style were around the table.

Jakon always sat on the newest. His chair it was. The smell bit his nose the strongest, like a dog nipping the nostrils, except with the smell of fresh wrought iron rather than with teeth.

A black iron bowl was already in front of his seat, and not just any bowl, but the bowls dad forged to match the black roses of this very table.

Something very special was going on ...

Something his parents hadn't told him about yet either ...

Even stranger, dad was seated at the table, and without any bowl or plate, but he despised strawberries with a passion. That bulging nose of his was curled wrinkled. It could be that strawberries were too close to him, but he wasn't the type to deny his son a good food simply because he disliked it.

Anyway, he was one of the stoutest dwarfs in all of Dirlop, and proud of it. His long black beard was braided among the thickest and trimmest too, and right now, it was over his dark gray smithery apron, which was as long as a full dress and thicker some most fabric-based armor ... but if he had his apron on ... he came here right from his smithery.

Jakon sat down anyway. Mom went through the effort too ...

Mom sat beside dad, and ... no bowl either. Or plate. And she just loooved these strawberries and cream. Why ... sigh. Let's say she was on the thinner side, and really could use a few desserts in her, but her face was lined with concern. Her blonde hair wasn't even braided, and that smile on her face missed her eyes by miles.

Jakon wasn't that clueless. This didn't look good. Better start the conversation first, or else–

"Thanks for the ... breakfast," Jakon said.

Dad hurrumpfed. "Yes, breakfast. Dessert for breakfast."

"*Honey*," mom said, "We spoke about this."

Dad merely nodded. Hurrumpfed again.

"We did," he said, "And agreed, but news from up north ... those orcs and their blasted dragon overlords already anointed their new–"

"**Not** in front of Jakon," mom said.

Dad hurrumpfed again.

"He'd old enough to hear it," dad said, "He's more than human enough. Almost a man now, if not already. His dwarf side's ... in spirit more than body."

That got dad a fierce glare from mom.

Jakon knew better than to jump in.

Yet.

Or start his strawberries and cream. Dessert for breakfast. A very bad sign indeed.

Jakon merely leaned back in his seat and waited for the right moment ...

Dad hurrumpfed once again, and he had won all the hurrumpfing contests for a hundred years straight. He was too proud of his hurrumpfs not to use them whenever he could, whether he should or not.

"The boy reads about those Seven Deadly Serpent wannabes in his blasted books," dad said, "The real thing's finally come about, rumor has it. They even selected another Princess of Smiles."

The Princess of Smiles ... of the bloody neck kind. Legend had it, back before she was killed with the rest of the Seven Deadly Serpents, she could wield up to a million blades through her mind and even use magical techniques through them like they were witch's staffs.

But that was thousands of years ago. What life was like back then ... the dime dreadfuls only pretended to know, and Jakon realized that much.

So he made a point to grimace, and nothing more.

But mom and dad were looking at him, and clearly for more than just the correct physical reaction ...

"It's bad news," Jakon said, "But my blades are ready if it comes down it to. Mom trained me well ... enough, right?"

Dad chuckled. "She's a blademaster, she is!"

"*Was,*" mom said, "And Jakon has a far way to go. Very far. I haven't figured out how to open his spores to magic."

Dad hurrumpfed. "Dwarves have no spores. Dwarf skin is the thickest and best there is!"

"The spores are spiritual, honey," mom said, "And I can sense them in him. The trouble has to do with his dwarven blood, so–"

"Blaming dwarfs for the boy's trouble, ey?" dad said, "As I see it, it's the other way around."

"I know you do, honey," mom said, "But that doesn't change the fact he needs training from someone besides me. Someone who–"

"Is too far away!" dad said, "No telling what horrors he'll run into on the road, and we can't come with him. He's not ready! Not alone he isn't."

That ... perked Jakon up. Traveling alone ... maybe not, but leaving Dirlop for an adventure ... maybe ... fun?

Maybe.

"Hooooney," mom said, "I've arranged for others to go with him. They'll arrive any day now–"

"Unless," dad said, "They were ambushed on the road. Orcs and worse are out there now. Too much for my son to fight off alone, and we can't spare the men to guide him, let alone watch over him. War's coming and–"

"Best he'd not in the middle of it," mom said, "If he's here ... he'll end up fighting before he's ready, and–"

"Enough!" dad said, "We agreed to disagree, ey? Let the boy decide. He'd old enough."

Mom and dad again both looked at Jakon and ... wow, ugh, was this ...

"Who and where and ... um," Jakon said.

More like sputtered.

Jakon cleared his throat. "I picked up some of what you're saying, but–"

"No means no, great!" dad said, "I knew you'd embrace your inner dwarf."

Mom tsked. "Give our boy a chance to speak for himself."

Oh well. Second try's as worthwhile as a first, as any dwarf knows.

"If ... I mean, with war coming ..." Jakon said, "I want to be as ready as possible, to fight. Dirlop is my home. Its safety is too important. Leaving that to everyone else? Of course not! That means being able to use magic with my sword tech-niques, even if my dwarf side ...a dwarf faces a challenge head on, and ... this morning, for a moment, I saw a castle on Razorspine Peak, before it disappeared."

"Castle?!" dad said, "Blast it! You've read so many of those dime–"

Jakon scowled this time. "A dwarf trusts his eyes."

Dad hurrumpfed, but ... nodded?

"True ..." dad said.

Mom even jumped in. "Jakon never told those tales like they were true."

"Not before ..." dad said, "**Fine.** I'll ask around. Even if it was there for only a moment, a few other dwarves should of seen it too."

Other dwarfs ... Jakon smiled a touch. Dad still saw Jakon as a dwarf.

Dad looked fierce at mom. "Let's hold off till I investigate this ... castle rumor, ey?"

Mom nodded. Her smile just as false now.

"It's for the best," mom said, "Jakon, we'll continue this at lunch."

'But ..." Jakon said, "At least–"

"Lunch!" both mom and dad said.

Sigh. A united front. No hope now of getting a full story out of them.

Leaving Jakon mostly in the dark ... again.

CHAPTER 3
JAKON

Now there was one last stone he could overturn and hopefully uncover whatever his parents had in store for him, but that stone was, in fact, a stout and very stubborn dwarf known as Rabbi Lam.

Even better, Jakon knew exactly where to find him at this time.

Usually.

As in most of the time.

The marketplace was vast round cavern full of the usual rubies and sparkling glowing gemstones. They were all colorful and all chiseled deep and into the spiky roof. The spikes always leaked into round smooth craters with clear ponds on the bottom. And those ponds were so colorful, deep and echoey that were pitch dark beyond a few, crystal blue paces. But despite a few attempts by children, no one ever swam in them, unfortunately. There were steps chiseled on the inside, just not on the outside wall. That wall was too tall and sleek to climb over, and the many countless slits through the wall were too thin even for Jakon to slip through ...

Or so everyone thought ... but everyone had their secrets.

But wow, was the water in them nice and cool on top, and a few paces below their surface, nice and steamy hot and refreshing.

More importantly, for the moment, by the pond with the most colorful rainbow of rings along the sides, and at one of the best locations because so many hallways went right passed it, was one of the best caves for a shop.

From the outside it looked like a huge round boulder had been chiseled right out, but that was only because there was a massive column in the center. The column led around the shop in a deceptively simple loop except ... it was dark. Enough that even a dwarf with good mining sight would need to squint. The whole shop was dark. The gemstones in the ceiling weren't shining at all? And the shop was barred with black iron.

Closed?

That's unusual. It was usually opened by now.

"Jakon!"

"Gunter!" Jakon said.

Trotting with serious effort but clearly refusing to show it, Gunter was a stout young dwarf but on the thinner side, but like a true dwarf, he didn't hesitate to marched right up to Jakon. In his hands was a crate of hefty books printed by his dad's press and that crate was giving him the trouble. No doubt he was busy delivering everyone's book orders for the day. He was mature for his age, but often in the wrong way …

"See Rabbi Lam today?" Gunter said, "I've got to drop these prayer books off pronto or else …"

"Sorry," Jakon said, "I came to see him too. Check the temple yet?"

"Yeah," Gunter said, "He's not there either. It's all closed up even!"

They both sighed together.

Gunter hurrumpfed, but clearly, he needed more practice compared to dad.

"Ordering books and not being there to receive them …" Gunter said, "He even said not to let any of them touch the ground so I can't just leave them here … do me a favor. If you find Rabbi Lam, give him a knock on the head and tell him his prayer books are back at storage."

"Will do," Jakon said, "If I see him, and … by the way, were you … when the sun was rising today … did you … see anything on Razorspine Peak?"

"Up and working long before sunrise," Gunter said, "Lucky you got to sleep in. But what did you see? You know I love your stories … it's only a matter of time before I can get my dad to print them in–"

"It's not a story," Jakon said, "I really saw … something."

"Ha!" Gunter said, "I love your angle. Finally going for that real touch rather than 'I just heard it from someone no one could of ever met'."

"No no," Jakon said, "I really did see something–"

"That's the spirit!" Gunter said, "Never let them think it's made up! I've got to go but–"

"Wait wait wait," Jakon said, "You see a castle–"

"A castle?" Gunter said, "In these parts? Ha! Good one! Make sure to throw in some monsters in the telling. No castle story's good without some good monster scares. Now I've got to get going ..."

Jakon sighed. Nodded.

"I'll let Rabbi Lam know," Jakon said, "If I see him. Big if."

"I know, I know," Gunter said, "I won't tell a soul about that castle story–yet. It definitely needs some polish, but it holds promise. Lots and lots of promise. Did you read that *Blood Rose of Doom* book that just came out? I know you have a copy."

"Not yet," Jakon said, "It's next on the to-read list. I've got to get going. Training you know, and–"

"I know, I know," Gunter said, "Heard the monster races are up to no good again. If dwarves like you aren't in top shape ... too bad a few books their way wouldn't ... no, monsters are monsters, through and through."

They both nodded.

Gunter even grinned sneaky.

"That's why carding them is so great," he said, "Might as well put them to good use!"

Jakon sighed. "You've got some new awesome card to show me, don't you?"

Monster carding was ... killing monsters, even darklings, and then binding their spirits to a card made from the right kind of alchemy. All so that they can be summoned and commanded like devoted pawns, but, of course, the materials of the card itself limited their combat potential, and the compulsion to obey as well, so forget becoming a warlord by collecting a bunch of monster cards.

Still, monster carding was great for storing them as fresh materials for smithing, alchemy, and, of course, Jakon gave up collecting back when ... sigh, Gunter and Jakon used to dwarf-to-dwarf team up against other dwarf teams with monster card battles and sigh.

No.

"Exactly," Gunter said, "Remember the old days, collecting them and fighting together with them? It's time to start a good habit anew! See my Orb-Eyed Coral Crisis Snake!"

The card was the size of a playing card. On front was a snake the length of their leg and a quarter as thick, but all clearly muscle. Its rainbow coloring was crazy bright and its single huge eye was a spooky bright coral blue.

Before Jakon could say anything Gunter held the card out and said, "Come forth, Minion of my will!"

PUFF!

A rainbow-colored puff of smoke as tall as his waist and just as wide, and woh, did it smell serpenty and yet, watery and salty too. Like one of the occasional long-lost artifacts supposedly fished out from the sea far away and brought here to Dirlop Mountain and sold to his dad, or to the dwarven alchemists.

The puff suddenly condensed into an eight-foot-long snake. Exactly what was pictured on the card.

It hissed, and swayed to its own internal song, but its serpent eye was utterly blank and mindless.

Gunter laughed like a mad man. "You've got to see how one of these babies deals with an orc!"

Before Jakon could protest. Gunter already summoned an orc with a big puff. A green cloud that smelled so warthoggish piggish and condensed into a man-shaped warthog with green skin and full leather armor of the raggiest, smelliest sort. An orc soldier complete with pair of black-bladed scimitars.

Gunter laughed again. "Witch is the *Best!*"

The orc bellowed.

Attacked.

The snake hissed.

Dodged.

Its eye glowed. Bright pale blue. Sparkled.

The orc squealed.

Shocked still.

Just as the snake lunged. Shoved itself down the orc's throat.

The orc shuttered. Dropped dead.

Puff!

One card? Same warthoggish orc, but now ... underneath the picture, it's breed: A Crisis Controlled Soldier Orc?

What the ... what was that?

Jakon knew better than to ask. He had one more stop today before training today, and a secret one at that, so ...

"Exactly," Jakon said, "Got to go, *now.* Sorry ... blademaster teachers can be real harsh about lateness and ..."

"One more card,' Gunter said, "and you'll love this one. I guarantee it!"

Jakon sighed. "*Fine*. One more. And that's it."

"Perfect!" Gunter said and flicked another card out.

His perverted grin already set Jakon and his own heart to cringe.

"Come forth," Grunter said, "Girl of my naughtiest dreams!"

Oh no ...

CHAPTER 4
AZURA

That's Azura's cue ...

Show time!

Azura let her card puff into the whitest of snow-white puffs of smoke. A full six feet high and couple paces wide, of course, so there would be plenty of room for her foxy tail as she swirled so sexy dainty cute, like the cute little fox girl she was—even if now she was all grown up, an eighteen-year-old beauty since last week!

Even if this twirl was her still basically chasing her own fox tail while spinning 'round and 'round on her two hindquarter paws. She twirled her fresh scent of clean crisp fox and snow around far and wide.

Yet the smoke still hid how her figure was now definitely like a full buxom-chested yet slim-bodied elf girl.

That dank touch to the air didn't bother her ... much.

Not anymore.

This was Dirlop Mountain, after all. As a vixen beast elf girl, a darkling elf no less, she was lucky to be here safe and sound, and not harvested for material, mainly her gorgeous sky-blue hair. Or worse, now that she was eighteen and fully grown in body and magic, her body parts were potent with enough magic to be worth harvesting and being forged into items like armor and weapons and more.

Thanks to Gunter *and* Mr Dawdora she could live out her days forever as a young, beautiful snow vixen elf monster girl card, and not some slaved soul inside some stupid item.

Her own free will fully intact.

Even within this misty cloud, and woh, the echoes from every which where, her magic kept her fur coat short and trim. It prevented it from getting soggy with dankness, and kept her nice and cozy—not too warm, not too cold.

It especially kept her fox ears perked high up and well out of her long wind-blown hair and how nice was it that the card ensured her hair grew trim and straight down beside her busty chest that Gunter couldn't help but ogle aaaaalllll the time and down to her slim waist that Gunter loved to scratch so tickly that–he-he, she cackled just thinking of his scruffy touch.

A touch he never forced on her either. No doubt he wanted to scratch her ears again or some like ...

The cloud vanished, and she was suddenly surrounded with darkness. A vast cavern? Phew.

Better another cavern than another night outside Dirlop Mountain.

Better keep an eye on her surrounds since in a game, no

telling if an enemy card master would try underhanded moves—like chucking a card somewhere she hadn't noticed and attack by surprise.

To her side tall walls blockaded some colorful pool that she sooo wanted to try diving into but nope, life as a card monster had its limitations.

But no attacks from that direction, at least.

To her other side, was an opening almost as tall as she was, but several paces wide, and ... no, it was barred. Sealed tight, and darker than her surroundings.

Her vision was picking up again and ... that tug from her heart, as a living card monster she could sense her master and ah!

Gunter was paces behind her.

Probably ogling her furry rear like usual, and hoping for an excuse to stroke her tail again, which, he-he, she'd so give him, once he fed her some more tasty sweet chicken jerky, that was.

Not that, as a card monster, she ever needed to eat. Not really. But she still enjoyed it.

She scented the air and ... warthoggish orc beside her, but that tug from it, it was wielded by Gunter, so no worries. He'd never fuse her, or do anything that she didn't approve of with her, and not just because a living monster card had more control of her fate than most card wielders realized.

In front of her was ...

Azura gasped. "Oh!"

A taaaaaallll handsome dwarf right before her, and she was now a solid six feet of height so his eyes were right perfect at her busty chest level–he-he–but his beard ... only black stubble?

Strange, but kinda cute, actually, with that chiseled face of a ... oh, a human warrior. And those strong gray eyes stared at her foxy snout and pink nose. He hadn't ogled her chest, as big and ogle worthy as it was.

(How annoying.)

He looked as solid as the stone floor beneath her paws, yet he had the lean and mean build of a human warrior too (and sooo tasty looking she even licked her chops!)

His scent, up her long foxy snout, ah!

Not just that oh-so-familiar bison-that-wasn't-bison scent, the scent of dwarfs, but a good hint of pig-that-wasn't-pig, but human.

He was a half-dwarf, half-human? Yay! He might just have the right mix of bearded delight with that human touch to enjoy all her forms. Her elf girl form with only fox ear and tail, and her vixen form with a fur coat, and foxy face and legs, oh, and *retractable* claws, which she could trim his beard once he actually grew one.

Let's stick with her vixen form for now. Even with her foot claws scratching up the stone floor as lightly as she could get away with, and wow, was the gemstone light so colorful and bright now.

(Dwarfs had so much wealth and didn't even realize it!)

That tall dwarf didn't even step back in shock like Gunter did the first time he summoned cute little her over a decade ago.

This tall dwarf just stood there. As solid as the stone of the very cavern.

So okay, she would stay bare in the fur. Gunter hadn't found the right kind of outfit for her yet anyway—in either of her forms, so bare peaches and cream delight ... nah, too sexy for these young cute dwarfs to handle.

(Best save *that* for the right moment.)

And her thick sky-blue belt of leather didn't count. Sure, it hung lopsided off her slim waist. Sure, it had that lovely heart-shaped pouch of lovely rosy pink on its lower side.

And her rosy-pink pair of dragon bone claw extenders also known as katars ... but nope, none of that counted as a real genuine outfit.

This tall dwarf was wearing a real genuine outfit. A lovely and revealing jerkin of dark blue leather along with a decent pair of dark slacks and solid thick boots.

Unlike her, who really was basically bare in the fur, all because Gunter, supposedly, couldn't find a compatible garb card to upgrade her with.

(Yeah. *Supposedly* ... not that she minded, much.)

"You must be that Jakon," Azura said, and scented him again and ah!

His crisp bison scent was mingled with solid streaks of biting hot iron—a Dawdora! Yay!

He must be that bestie Gunter told her all about. Dime dreadful addict, kinda like her, and used to be a monster card addict, until that fateful day when his half breed nature prevented him from using card smithing the dwarven way so no more dwarf smith future for him.

(Too bad.)

Jakon, that tall handsome dwarf, hurrumpfed so handsomely.

"Your eyes ..." Jakon said.

"As beautiful as the rest of me," Azura said, "I *so* know, but thanks for–"

"True but you're alive," Jakon said, "A living monster card. Keeping you bound like this isn't right. Gunter, explain yourself. Why haven't you freed her?"

Gunter chuckled. "Free her? Jakon ... Azura's as free as she can be!"

Azura huffed herself. She wasn't a dwarf so she'd never hurrumpf. Ever.

But her slim hands did fist her fantastic hips. As she jutted her them all out toward that cute little Jakon.

"Free me?" she said, "Gunter's right. Where would I go? Think, my dear dwarf."

Jakon hurrumpfed again. "I know you're a darkling. You'd flee to your Dragon Lords and go fodder witch for them. Against us. But keeping you slaved like this isn't right either–"

Azura cackled. "Slaved? Me? Nope. Try again."

Jakon hurrumpfed. Again. Wow. He must of proud of his hurrumpfs, but then again, she heard the Dawdoras were famous for them among dwarf kind

"A living monster card, forged properly, cannot be compelled so easily," Jakon said, "But there are still restrictions, based on the willpower of your wielder, and those restrictions–"

"Are less severe," Azura said, "than whatever I'd have to suffer under those Dragon Lords."

"Well ..." Jakon said.

That shock all over that warrior face ... he-he. She'd **so** have to slay him if she were free but since she was just a cute sexy monster card ...

"I *like* being a living monster card too," Azura said, "Some of us darklings *do* prefer it. Especially since we can't be used for alchemy parts, and ..."

Azura did her best not to shutter.

Or cringe.

At least back then the alchemists only wanted her hair. Not ... other parts of her.

(Yet.)

"I see," Jakon said, "I ..."

Azura hopped right into his arms. Smothered his face into her busty buxom because that's what they're there for. And there was nothing better than savoring his lusty shocked gasp right against the fluffy fur by her heart, between her breasts.

"My new master understands!" she said, "Yaaaayyyy! I just know you would. Now let Azura serve and pleasure you!"

"Mast—WHAT?!?!?" Jakon said.

He-he. Too shocked to resist her charm now too. Perfect!

Gunter chuckled, and (Azura peeking oh so slyly) that that sly little Gunter shoved something ... oh, a small box... as thick as his pinky ... a dozen card deck?!

Yay! She won't be alone for long.

"Got to start again somewhere," Gunter said, "The Crisis

Orc is in there too. It's far better any regular orc. It's a captain class card! Even if it can't command other cards—yet."

Azura giggled again. "And I'm the best of the best kind of card too!"

Jakon nodded, but was still too shocked to respond coherently.

Yay!

She'd so become his general card. Girlfriend general. Unlike Gunter, who was still too glued to dwarf women to embrace her charm completely, but this half breed Jakon had the perfect mix to fall for her.

Especially once she went bare nude elf girl in his lap and ... he-he.

Gunter chuckled. "She's more than looks too. Powerful beyond ... well, snow vixen witches aren't common for a real reason. She's a real rare of the rare sort. Her beauty ain't fur deep either. Thank the Light she's on our side, is all I'm saying. Take good care of her, Jakon. She can fight beside you like a familiar. In real battles–if you treat her right. She's a real battle bitch card, not that–"

"Aaaaawwwww," Azura said, "I'm sure my cute little master will sex me all right, right?"

"I'll–I'll–wait, *what?*" Jakon said.

"Or else my pair of busty scarlet vixen guards," Azura said, "will soooo punish you, right girls?"

CHAPTER 5
JAKON

"Yeah!"

Two girlie voices? From the box in his hand?!

Jakon. His face. It was smothered in furry breast beyond his wildest dreams, and and and ... no!

His boots were solid. On the ground. His strawberries and cream breakfast lingered in the back of his throat, and no, his parents would never approve of this ... smutty fox girl's behavior toward him, but with so many echoes in this cavern, no doubt word of this would reach his dad in no time, since there were other shops open and doing business and so many hurrumpfs echoing out around from beyond ... but Jakon, he ... he *enjoyed* smelling crisp clean fox girl, Light help him ... this boob face thing wasn't ... unpleasant, actually, and she was so very warm and soft compared to the cool air of the cavern, and better than ... nonono.

He hugged her tight. "Azura Return!"

Finally.

PUFF!

Azura returned to her monster card state, and damn, was she just as gorgeously sexy as she posed on her card as she was in giggling sultry real life.

Sigh. Release her and she would certainly become an enemy that needed killing. All three of them knew it and clearly she didn't want that as much as anyone else here did, so sigh.

Gunter and his more … perverted sense of the world … Jakon couldn't but Azura wanted it, and honestly, if Jakon was going to travel dangerous roads soon, some living monster cards willing to back him up … sigh.

"Thanks!" Jakon said, and headed off.

More like dashed off. Deck in hand anyway but hopefully Azura and her vixen guards wouldn't pop up out of nowhere … no. He still had enough control over when they could appear.

Or should.

"I can imagine the training will be harsh but … enjoy!" Gunter said, and headed the other way.

(Thank the Light.)

CHAPTER 6
JAKON

Now Jakon had time for one more stop, but it was tucked in a hard-to-reach part of Dirlop Mountain. The trail here itself was more of a rough deer trail than any kind of road. In fact, it was so thin it was the kind of trail only scrawny starved deer could hope to get through. To make matters worse, the trail went between countless boulders that were craggy and towering big. They were all light gray, almost as gray as the sky rumbling above him, and with plenty of false branches that led to nowhere, or worse, to a sudden steep cliff few dwarfs could hope to fall down and survive.

Oh, and don't forget the couple of craggy boulders crudely bridging a deep, dark chasm.

Or the craggy head-shaped boulders that provided stepping stones to hop over another deep, dark, and *very* echoey chasm.

But only a lean and mean kind of guy could hope to traverse this trail, so very, *very* few people in Dirlop could follow him here, had they even known about it, which almost no one did.

Almost.

It was their secret little spot, pretty much, and his breakfast of strawberries and cream was powering him extra fast through it today.

Since right now, there was nowhere else he would rather go than this very hot spring, or pond, or maybe it was both, but it was at the end of this winding, dangerously thin trail.

The hot spring's water was amazingly clear and stunningly clean, at least the surface, but both above and below the surface, there were more craggy boulders from house-cat sized to towering huge. Some made awesome seats. Some made makeshift floors—as long as you watched out for the many, many underwater crevices into the dark, deep depths, but swimming over them, as spooky as the darkness was below, no problem.

But best of all, that hint of orange and cream, as embarrassing as that scent was to the source ... the purr the moment he arrived ... Ivy Reap.

She looked like a tigermite i.e. human girl with her skin colored like an orange tiger, and with house-cat ears poking out of her windblown scarlet hair. Her tiger tail always even wiggled like it had a mind of its own.

Except she was more beautiful than any human girl could hope to become. Her figure was so curved slim in the rightest way, and curved obese in the chest places. It was so big it shocked him the first time seeing it. He had too much trouble not leering at it. And throw in her orange and cream scent ... she was definitely half elf girl.

Crouched on top of a towering-high mouse-shaped boulder mere paces ahead of him, Ivy wore form-fitting slacks that left just enough to the imagination and cowled bra top that left even less to the imagination. Both were as scarlet bright as her long ponytailed hair, and her garb was full of shiny bone studs carved into little tiny human skulls.

But her those big bright green eyes staring super happy at him.

Her fanged grin might of spooked less worthy men, like elves, but not–

"Jakon!" Ivy said, "Time to ... spare!"

She whipped out her steel katars. Which looked like steel knuckles except that instead of steel knobs for the knuckles, both had long thick steel blades.

And she leapt.

Pouncing him.

His training took over. Just as her katars came within reach of his chest. He caught her arms.

Rolled backwards.

Gently shoving his thick leather boots into her soft exposed belly.

Rolling over with him she giggled.

Laughed.

And she plopped solid on the ground beyond his head. The top of their heads were next to each other, and they held hands now and wow, did Ivy have such soft hands. Even with her retractable claws, she never scratched him badly with them, and wow, could she slash someone bad with them, if she wanted to.

Ivy took a deep breath. "If we ever fought for real ..."

"I would *sooo,*" Jakon said, "go pervy dwarf on you. Those boobs would be sooo groped it wouldn't be–"

"Funny?" Ivy said, "I have *great* boobs! Perfect for that deadly distract and slash."

"Exactly," Jakon said, "Ever consider fighting naked? You've practically halfway there ..."

"Ooo," Ivy said, "I would *sooo* wear a skirt. A supershort skirt, and kick a lot. Last glance down there will be *your* **last!!!**"

They both giggled this time. Still holding hands, and loving it, yet ... Jakon ... he had to ...

"Ivy," Jakon said, "there's something else I need to tell you."

"Ooo," Ivy said, "Time for our first actual date? I did say you have to defeat me first. It's a tigermite mate thing, you know, without actually hurting me, and no excuses, you clutz! Or else you *so* will discover why tigermite girls are feared among our men ... he-he."

"No no, that's not – wait, what?" Jakon said, still holding her hands, but the smooth stone ground against his back now felt too solid, too wet.

"You heard me," Ivy said, "But I scent another girl on you so ..."

"That's what I wanted to talk about," Jakon said, and squeezed her hands tenderly, even if her fingertips pricked him with her claws, "Gunter gave me a dozen card deck of monster cards, and one of them is a living monster card. A gorgeous and feisty snow vixen elf named Azura, and she–"

"Ooo," Ivy said, "Not a date but a carding then? Fine. *If* you defeat me. I'll go be one of your living monster cards. But only if you defeat. If I defeat you, it's—he-he—you become my living monster card. Fair's fair, right?"

"Right that's—wait, *what?!*" Jakon said, "Why are you … so alright with being carded?"

"A girl just *loooves* being cherished," Ivy said, "And a living monster card of the true battle type is truly cherished, and yes, I'm only accepting a true battle type carding. None of this playing card nonsense only stuff 'cause living monster cards *have* to be true battle types."

"You mean," Jakon said, "True Monster Cards."

"Oh yeah, *that,*" Ivy said, "The kind that can be used for fighting, not just fighting enhancements."

"Enhancements?" Jakon said, "You mean …"

"Us magical critters," Ivy said, "Get enhancements holding the right number and kind of monster cards—*if* they're made right, which is hard, even for dwarfs to get right, and that's saying something, but really, why do you think they're so popular? Really … sorry, Jakie Poo. You're dwarf and human, so twice the nonmagical sorry for you there."

"And living monster cards," Jakon said, "Are harder for fighters like us to defeat. Imagine the abuse–"

"Don't need to imagine," Ivy said, "Plenty of card collectors have come after me, and lots and lots of nations raise battle hungry monsters all to card them into war decks wielded by their nobles or generals and blah blah blah. Monsters like me are in such hiiiiigh demand, it's scary sometimes."

Jakon sighed. "Ever wonder what would happen if us lightlings could be carded too?"

"Ooo," Ivy said, "What a dream come true! Less demand for us darkling monsters. Yay!"

"No," Jakon said, "Even more, I think. Any petty noble would create a war deck, so guys like me would be carded as their fodder, well, if I lived elsewhere, maybe, but it's monsters like you and stronger that would become even more important. The tie breakers."

"Well ..." Ivy said.

"Think about it," Jakon said, "It's one of the reasons petty nobles don't have war decks. Just the deck itself is pricy but that's not enough to stop small decks being built, except each monster carding is just as incredibly expensive, so only people with real wealth or connections could hope to create a deck of True Monster Cards. But if regular folk like us could be carded, enhanced, then small decks of regular enhanced folk would become far more common."

"Ooo ... crap," Ivy said, "You're right. That ... nonono. That has to be wrong but ..."

"Sorry, Ivy," Jakon said, "But I'm ... flattered you're so willing to go living monster card for me. It's tempting, in a sense, since I know ... well ... a deck of Living Monster Cards ... well ..."

Ivy purred. "Well, what? You going somewhere? Leaving poor little me behind?"

'Um," Jakon said, "Maybe. Not sure yet. The parental units are undecided, and in conflict, but I suspect it's only a matter of time, all because of spores or something."

"Ooo," Ivy said, "You mean magical spores? You have them too? Yay! Once you open them ... wait ... why haven't yours opened, if you have them?"

"Good question," Jakon said, "And I don't know. That's why my mom wants to send me to someone who might be able to help me with that but my dad's ... reluctant, and after I saw that strange castle on Razorspine Peak for a–"

"*You* TOO?!?!?" Ivy said, and from holding hands and on her back, she flipped over, over him and landed her fine sexy ass right over his gut and now her awesome sexy legs vised his chest.

The impact of sexy left Jakon breathless, especially with the smooth hard stone against his back, but seeing Ivy stare so bright-eyed intent down at him—despite her amazingly ample chest taking up most of his view of her.

Even with her vicing his chest with those amazing legs of hers ...

Her grinning so kitty cute fanged at him ... Jakon only managed to smile big back at her, and not heat up redder than iron in a smithy fire.

"I soooo saw it too!' Ivy said, "*Sooo* spooky. I so want to explore it but ... let's go together!"

Now, Jakon couldn't help but grin more than ... heart-thumping happy.

"Traveling together ..." Jakon said, but couldn't finish after Ivy laughed so happy her amble chest jiggled cheek warmingly amazing.

"Better than alone," she said.

"Much better."

And heading into a dangerously fun and looong journey ... never sounded better.

CHAPTER 7
FROSTINE

The death of that dwarf still unsettled Frostine so much she couldn't savor her paltry lunch of deliciously salty chicken jerky, and chicken jerky was second to chicken soup to tummy yummy perfection, and yet … no, she mustn't sip any of the chicken soup from her canteen … for now.

As the most powerful snow vixen witch here in this squad, she got to sit on the most comfortable boulder, of course, and it was the very same boulder, amazingly flat and smooth yet cupping her furry butt perfectly, and more than low enough to be cozy, despite below her knees being like the hindquarters of a large fox, and it was the same boulder that the now dead dwarf had been seated on, staring off at …

Uh huh.

That really towering high and craggy mountain off in the

awfully blue distance ... as blue as too many called her own eyes, and ugh, she almost hated blue because of that.

Almost.

Strange how that lone mountain was just there. In the middle of that thick murky forest full of steep craggy cliffs and even more jagged boulders, and so many wild vicious tigermites that held no allegiance to anyone, even the Dragon Lords, but once this Dirlop Mountain was conquered, they'd join the Dragon Lords and continue the conquest, since this Dirlop Mountain was right in the middle of a critical trade route for the whole continent.

But still, where all these jagged boulders came from ... la sigh.

None of her business. Once her time as a witch trooper was over, she could look into it. Later. The Dragon Lords had libraries like human farms had chickens and cows.

She even leaned back some, let the smell of that vanquished dwarf ... the thick smell of bison that wasn't bison, but actual real dwarf, the scent lingered up throughout her whole entire snout, but as a beast elf of the snow vixen variety, her ice and lightning magic was second to none, so freezing that dwarf, shattering him into nothingness before he had a chance to strike.

Perfect first kill.

Yes.

Perfect. Her twin sis Pearl would be so proud of her too.

Yet her heart still thunked so fast so far after the danger was passed ... her foxy tail limped so sad over the back of this rock ... even her ears didn't perk up as high, and her fox ears loved to perk up from the slightest bit of an excuse.

Like how proud she should be. Her strike was so good, there was no chance of that dwarf even got the chance to see who killed him. And that was despite how the boulders surrounding this nice cozy seat of a boulder were easier to climb from the outside in than from the inside out.

It would also become the perfect trap—for later.

With her white fur coat, she blended in halfway well with some of the lighter gray boulders too, even if it was kinda hot, her magical powers kept her comfy and amazingly clean, despite the crazy amount of dust every which where. But right now, she better be wary of how easy it would be for some enemy dwarf to sneak up on her here. How many times had Drakoth, her dragon instructor, sneaked up her and he was several times bigger than the biggest stallion?

But here, and now, Frostine was far from alone.

So she even leaned back and la sighed again. Trying to relax some before the coming battle.

But the foxy scent of her companions ... especially the red fox boy standing behind her, standing slim but wiry, and in black slacks that matched his red fox fur perfectly, and his own black iron claw extenders. He didn't even let Frostine know his name. Yet.

He just stood tall and silent behind her. Ready, just like the guard she had sent on a secret mission.

She crossed her legs nice and sexy for her remaining bodyguard guy. Just like Pearl would of done, he-he. Both bodyguards were slim yet muscular fox elf guys, but her other guard was away, inside the mountain, executing another plan of hers.

But any fox boy would definitely of appreciated a vixen girl like her. All her forms were humanoid, like most beast elves, and those who had full beast forms, they often were trained as scouts and so on, not as witches or guards.

So to be ready for battle, Frostine stayed in her vixen form, of course, so below her knees, like the hindquarters of a canine, and her hands, well, better keep them with their deadly claws out fully.

It was what Pearl always did, and Drakoth never managed to surprise Pearl like he did Frostine. Pearl always claimed it was because her long lush hair was so platinum pink rather than pale sunny golden like Frostine's, and dragons so loved golden hair of any color that ... la sigh.

No, that couldn't be it.

Lucky them even received real armor, thanks to Drakoth. Both sets of armor were made out of the thick, pale blue bones of their own gigantic venomous snake. A pair of snakes that Drakoth himself caught and killed. One snake for each snow vixen student.

Her snake's skull was forged into her helm, and fit snug and perfect. It even had extra slits for her pointy ears to move around. Her waist long hair was neatly tucked underneath the helm but over the spine that connected it to the rest of the suit, including ribs that protected her chest, and her biggest weak point, her heart, but wow, did the extra-large size of her chest make that extra beefy and warthog-faced orc of an alchemist smith grumble at how much he needed to "adjust" those chest ribs.

Pearl had cackled so much at that grumbling ... Frostine even ended up giggling some too but ...

That alchemist orc even admitted to removing some ribs below their chest armor for material, and exposing more than their tummies should be. Far more, and that was with big red Drakoth watching over and ready to provide the extra powerful flames needed to forge both armors. The alchemist smith had even shortened the skirt, also made of ribs, but they were now far too short. Those ribs barely covered her down to the middle of her thighs.

Pearl loved showing off her figure, but she had a more than a few boys trying to snag her as their alpha mate already. Frostine was too busy to even notice if ... well, of course, a few did try to date her, but no time for dates.

Not with all that training. How Pearl managed to find the time ...

So no wonder her tail was so limp, but nothing she could do about it. Not now.

Sure, Frostine had regenerative healing, like all beast elves, but this pale blue armor of bone reduced it drastically, all so that she could receive a big boost in magical power. More than enough to shatter the dwarven battlements with bolts of lightning, and have plenty left over to ravage their small army just by herself. Make Drakoth proud.

When the time came ... Pearl would be ready to strike from behind, the opposite side of the mountain.

Both Frostine and Pearl better be ready to freeze those

inevitable waves of dwarven warriors into blocks of snazzy vixen-shaped ice.

Shatter that sexy shaped ice into naughty nothingness.

Something Pearl even loved to practice on the rodents scampering around at night. Like Pearl always told her, they both were six feet of deadly beauty, so better be proud of it and ... la sigh.

Pearl, even more so, with that lovely pink hair.

At least Frostine wasn't alone here. Or even the only vixen, even if she was the only snow vixen in this squad. Pearl was leading her own squad from behind Dirlop Mountain.

Instead, Frostine had Rubica and Sapphira, who were amazingly talented scarlet vixens, like red fox versions of a snow vixen, so their magic was all fire based but unlucky for them, no armor. Just black short skirts and short cowled bra tops.

Along with, of course, black iron claw extenders.

Just because Drakoth gave them some training, it wasn't nearly as much as Frostine and Pearl received.

Frostine had cute but sinister claw extenders too. Strapped to her waist, opposite of her pale blue pouch and its precious contents. Her claw extenders could hook onto her claws and could extend them for over a few more deadly razor feet.

They both were made from the same pale-blue bone of her serpent skeleton armor. She could also yank the fangs from her helm to use as throwing daggers, and the fangs would regrow and could be thrown again and again, as long as she didn't use up too much of her stamina. Something

Pearl still struggled with. She just loooved to throwing her helm's daggers too much. La sigh.

All that training from Drakoth … all for this first battle.

And many to come.

Pearl had been so excited and eager to do her part in this upcoming battle. She had wanted to do the frontal assault, but no, Drakoth chose Frostine to lead the frontal assault, and Pearl to lead the assault from behind.

A pincher attack, of sorts.

Even if their orc armies were contained entirely in a monster card deck. These were no ordinary monster cards. They could truly fight living people. Kill living people. It was a deck forged from countless orcs killed by those awful lightlings, and now giving their spirits a chance to avenge their own deaths.

How great was that!

Yet she … she'd need to kill far more dwarfs than the one she already took out.

And without hesitation.

Without a laugh, giggle, or … the witty comments Pearl always had ready.

Now strutting in front of her now, Rubica and Saphira, her two scarlet vixen elves, and clearly all ready to back her up, as their duty required.

Ready to die to protect her.

Rubica tsked, grinning wide, with her white fangs shining in the blazing sun. Huffing her small but cute chest out at one of her silent guards. Clearly testing the last guard's resolve not to be distracted by his sexy vixen wards.

"It's almost time," Rubica said, "Drano, at noon–"

Frostine huffed an extra loud la sigh. The scent of that fox boy ... his interest wasn't in vixens, or girls of any sort.

(Figures.)

"Rubica," Frostine said, "I am quite capable to leading this battle, no?"

"I ..." Rubica said, "That dwarf. We all saw how he took a toll on you. As your first kill."

Saphira flicked her long flowing cherry hair to the side, and huffed her chubby chest out and strutted tall and cocky over, right beside Rubica. Saphira was build slim but amazingly busty. Eye catching, and Drano, by his foxy smell, wow, he clearly enjoyed her presence.

So maybe he did enjoy both genders ... in that way.

"You trained so much," Saphira said, "You never had the chance to–"

Frostine huffed even louder. "So? I vill kill as I must. Zee dwarf is dead. Soon the rest vill join him. At highest noon I shall blast the battlements, no? Wipe out the first few waves of–"

"No!" Rubica said, and even grabbed Frostine's snout shut?

La sigh. Drakoth never taught them to respect their captain. Did Pearl have the same trouble with her scarlet vixens? Only the snow vixens held the orc decks. Only they had enough magic and stamina to wield the cards all at once.

Saphira even grumbled, hands on overnice hips. Her bright violet gaze so ... intense. Too much like Pearl's, even if Pearl's was as blue as Frostine's.

"Leave the first waves of dwarfs to us," Saphira said, "We're vixen witches too. Lower ranked, but we're a team, remember? Just because you're the captain ... with the orc deck ..."

Rubica nodded? Flicked her short wavy amber hair aside.

"**Captain** Frostine," Rubica said, "Don't try to do it all by yourself. *Please.* Leave some for the rest of us. Especially the orcs. They'll be so ... upset if you take out too many at first. They want their revenge, right? Right."

Frostine jerked her snout out of Rubica's grip, but ... as their leader ... doing everything ... la sigh. She did read dime dreadfuls of both sides, as naughty as that sounded, and leaders who do too much ...

"Fine," Frostine said, "I shall first destroy zee battlements. Our orcs shall then invade and vee shall follow up in zee rear. Sound good?"

Both Rubica and Saphira nodded. Perking up too.

Phew.

Frostine let herself grin a touch. "And I shall expose myself zee whole time. Attack here and there. Force zee dwarfs to come for me, no? Perfect way to–"

Saphira cackled all wicked.

"Exactly!" she said, "With us to help you, the dwarfs will have to focus on *us*, not the orc horde. Perfect!"

Her fox guard cleared his throat.

"My protection order only extends to the snow vixen," Drano said, "If the dwarfs reach us, then you both must be ready to die to protect Frostine as well. If Frostine dies, the deck and its orcs shall be vanquished, and we all are as good as dead, if not worse."

Worse ... as in material to be forged into talismans.

Both Rubica and Saphira nodded anyway. Even if Saphira seemed a touch annoyed by it, and the sour touch to her foxy scent confirming it.

Yet Saphira spoke first?

"I. am. *ready,*" Saphira said, "These dwarfs ... they call us monsters but they, they used *both* my sisters! Like, like as material to forge magical blades! They ... my sisters were just cublings and ..."

That scent? Such serious anger. Oh no.

Frostine hopped up and hugged Saphira. Anger would get her killed. Drakoth always defeated them when any of them got too angry.

Angry like that.

"They'll pay," Frostine said, "Zee arts of monster carding and alchemy shall be no more. Just like zee lightlings vill be."

Saphira hugged her back. "I know ... I know ... my sisters, even if they live, they aren't ... what they could of been. They're just ... just ..."

"Ooo, my third guard, Ramsel," Frostine said, "is already inside, posing as a vood elf, of course, and ready to ... he-he, guess what ... you won't believe it."

Both her scarlet vixens gasped at what she said next. Drano to chuckle nice and sinister.

And proud.

Those dwarves ... he-he. It even made Saphira hug her back extra snuggly.

Make Drano smell a touch sour from jealousy?

Now Frostine didn't have anything personal against these dwarfs–except they'd no doubt come after her, Pearl, and any other vixen given the chance. Turn them into monster cards or, worse, material for their dwarven alchemy. They already proved they'd go after scarlet vixens like Saphira and her little identical cubling sisters.

And for that, they had to die. Die before they killed Frostine and any more of her beloved beast elves.

Before the monster races were wiped out ...

The only way was for the dwarves to become livestock for dragon kind, as they deserved–for making her Saphira so ... furiously sad.

And ... for slaving the identical sister Frostine and Pearl would never know, except by name: Azura ... for the stunningly gorgeous sky-blue hair she was born with ...

And monster carded for.

CHAPTER 8

JAKON

Before Jakon knew it, he was already back at his mom's blademaster academy, but the clanks from countless blades hitting each other, hmmm, today those sounds sounded ... different, for some reason, yet he couldn't point his finger on how.

Yet.

First lesson of the basics was to double check his surroundings. Pay attention to what was around him, so let's see ...

The floor of his training room was the usual smooth yet gripping dark granite. The walls were mattressed thick with regenerating cushioning fashioned by the best dwarven alchemist and the high ceiling was flat yet glowed full of countless gemstones like most rooms throughout the mountain city of Dirlop did.

Nothing unusual there. Nothing to make those clanks ... different. Somehow.

The arched doorway ahead of him should lead to wider and busier but otherwise similar rooms than this one, but the arched doorway behind him, where he came from, was from a narrow granite hallway that circled the whole place. It was only used by some of the better students when they trained alone here, and only if they didn't want to disturb the other students if they arrived or left at different times than the lesser skilled students still in classes.

In fact, with the taste of strawberries and cream in the back of this throat, and the lingering memory of Ivy's orange and cream scent, and the softness of her hands and how warmly they touched his ... sigh.

Sure, tigermites in the forests below weren't thought well of, but they rarely joined up with other darklings to cause trouble for lightlings. They harassed everyone equally, so to speak, and dwarves here just happened to be close enough to get the brunt of it, but not all tigermite were ... unpleasant.

Ivy, for instance, yet the thought she could get monster carded ...

But even Ivy knew better than to show her face around any other dwarf. Too many were too stubbornly against tiger-mites of any sort. Some of the alchemist might even use her for parts to make their magical gadgets and trinkets. Of course, most alchemists preferred their material monster carded first. For easy storage and summoning. The very reason few beast elves of any allegiance ever showed up in

Dirlop Mountain except as cards to be used as material for alchemists and smiths forging magical objects.

That Ivy was almost always around that hot spring nearly every morning …

No.

Focus on why those clanks were … off. Not on Ivy. On whatever she might be doing when he was gone.

What she was never going to tell him.

Jakon had his pair of steel sabers, points and edge dulled, of course, since they were practice blades, of course, so they were a good bit extra heavy as well, to strength his arms as much as possible.

So all in all, he was ready to go through the exercises alone. All to cover for his lateness, and then join the others but … the clanks, there were no cries of pain. No smell of blood or injury.

Just lots of panting and determined huffs.

Enough that Jakon risked running through a few of the usual exercises extra hard to build up a sweat. To hide the fact he arrived late.

The usual lateness. Since Ivy needed a reason to come every day, and he needed a reason to see her every day and … sigh.

Mom would not be happy but … time to finally check out the main classroom.

CHAPTER 9
IVY

Ivy just looooved that wonderful blend of bison and pig that was neither, that was, in fact, her beloved sweet Jakon, and how did his scent make more than just her purr for more, and not just her tummy either.

This hot spring was like the find of a lifetime, all in itself. The way it weaved around so many of this huuuuge boulders and how so many of these boulders were exposed and craggy and so easy to climb around, yet they were so much like the countless boulders at home in the valley below this lone mountain.

So many boulders poked out of the hot spring. So many were completely submerged within the hot spring. It was obvious just looking at it, the spring went deep.

Maybe even deeper than mountain's own roots.

Underwater there were even minnows, and even bigger fish. More dangerous creatures. Plant monsters that resembled blue water lilies that ate the fish like venus fly traps eat flies.

Even eat her ... if she wasn't careful during her deeper dives.

But this time she brought talismans for both light *and* protection, which included near endless breath holding. They were both bracelets wore on each wrist and they were woven with water-proofed silk so very, very fragile, but very, very worth it.

She'd find another way into Dirlop Mountain. Another way to ... you know, sneak in, just like her elder wanted her to find, as an excuse to get her out of their village while the Dragon Lords tried to recruit their best warriors for dragon craziness.

Let alone carded like her brother was for ... you know. Dragons were just as bad as the ancient overlords that made tigermites as fodder for whatever stupid schemes blah blah blah.

Of course, she hated lying to Jakon. He was so trusting. So sweet. Just like his human mother, Helga. Who even trained Ivy a good little bit each day. Long after Jakon showed up each day.

As if Ivy was only Jakon's secret.

Ha!

But Dirlop Mountain was an eyesore to her kind. Well, most tigermites, at least. Dwarfs infesting key tigermite terri-tory ... (but honestly, better dwarfs than beast elves, orcs, dragon overlords and ugh.)

So if today's invasion of orcs and beast elves and ... other things succeeded ... tigermites would so be forced to go minion for those awful dragons.

Again.

And those snow vixen witches were scary good at magic. They snagged several of her village's best warriors. Defeating them all at once. Carding them in a monster deck.

A special deck. Meant for real, actual war.

But lucky for Ivy those vixens hadn't noticed her so far away and hidden. Or they didn't care.

Hopefully this next dive proved what she suspected true. Only one dive needed to succeed.

And with her luck ... this one would be it. A way to help the dwarves—and without being caught—he-he.

CHAPTER 10

JAKON

The moment Jakon entered the main classroom—an extra big and round room with thick cushioned regenerative walls—he was relieved he hadn't slacked off in his blademaster training, despite coming late nearly every day due to having secret fun with sexy cute Ivy, he did stay here later to make up for it ... usually.

Yet Jakon was very aware of the empty arched doorway behind him, this time.

Of the dome of a ceiling high above him. Of its many, many glowing gemstones keeping this extra big classroom extra bright and shadow-free.

The thick smell of sweat pierced through the hot air, and unsettled his breakfast of strawberries and cream, despite how familiar the sweat smell was, his breakfast was too sweet for this kind of smell.

At least his jerkin and slacks were woven with a layer of

protective lamia scales within them. His dad bought the half-dead pair of lamia elves off some merchants ages ago. In fact, his mom had an even better quality bright red dress that was woven from even higher grade and incredibly soft and silky lamia scales that were still amazingly protective.

His boots thwacked the floor. A floor wet with sweat and effort.

But a dozen paces ahead of him, a bunch of young chubby dwarves were gathered around a lean and mean guy with … five sabers floating around him? Strange, but Jakon heard of such ability before just, he never saw it in person, only read about it.

This guy had to be a sword swarm mage.

He had the ability to summon and command swords with his mind, yet … this new guy's ears … wait, his big triangular ears stuck out the sides of his short straggly blond hair like they were triangular daggers that would perk up and down like cat ears.

And the smell … a musk of something sweet and stomach tugging, in a good way, like candy of some sort. A milky creamy candy saved only for the best occasions, but also a hint of a bittersweet nip that nudged the stomach in a twisted way.

A real true elf guy?!?!

And a sword swarm mage.

Jakon already heard his heart go thump thump thump several times faster and louder. Too much like a fight he really might not win. A critical fight. The kind that hadn't happened to him in a while.

Except against his own mom.

But just as Jakon reached the edge of the ring of dwarfs, the elf guy said, "Thank you, I truly appreciate the honor of demonstrating my abilities to you, but that's all for today. I must go and ..."

"One more time!" a young dwarf said, "Please, Ramsel? It's Jakon! Our best just arrived!"

The elf guy called Ramsel sighed, grimaced.

"Sorry," Ramsel said, "I must go now. My work is almost done but ..."

Another young dwarf called out. "Show him your orcubus archer card!"

All the other dwarves cheered. "Show him!"

And their sneaky grins. Yikes.

Jakon shook his head. His heart pounding too fast.

This was too much like the last day he ever went into dad's smithy. He hadn't touched a monster card since–until today and ... ugh.

Best not dwell on his new deck of ... whatever. A living monster card, he'd have to take good care of her. Of them. Duty as a dwarf to do the right thing and ... well ...

Ramsel seemed to notice Jakon's hesitation.

"Best face your fears head on," Ramsel said, "I've healed her, again, but her tendency to disobey ..."

All the dwarfs chuckled, stroked their beards, and ugh. They all knew Jakon's ... fondness for the idea of elf girls compared to, well, dwarven women., and an orcubus was basically, well, the sexy of the most buxom yet slim elf girl, but combined with warthoggish warrior orcs so that ... no, just no.

"Monsters are bound to the will of the card wielder," Jakon said, "Any weakness in your will–"

"My will," Ramsel said, "is stronger than dwarven steel. I suspect the card is defective."

More than a few dwarves chuckled. So many young dwarves say that about their monster card training ... until they develop their own steel will, and their monster started behaving themself.

Jakon nodded. There was an obvious way to test it.

But Ramsel spoke first. Again?

"She is the only card of mine that dares defy me," he said.

And then he flicked the card over to Jakon?

"You may have her," Ramsel said, "As a gift. *If* you can control her better than me."

All the dwarfs chuckled and, oh no, those mumbles, chings of coin, they were gambling on the outcome.

And they were betting on him. Dwarves were a loyal lot, of course, so no chance they'd gamble on the newcomer.

So Jakon nodded. Looked at the card and ... oh crap.

She was ... drop dead *deadly* gorgeous. Bright red skin as smooth and brilliant as ... as ... a rising sun of ... *gulp*.

She was curved slim in the right places and obese in the chest places ... with long lush cherry hair straight down to her slim waist, and ... gulp.

She wore a cowled bra top and short *short* skirt. Both made of bright violet and incredibly shiny scales. They even had a curvy flowery trace of a pink heart over each boob and her crotch, and those scales, very form-fitting, and no doubt they were from a human-sized serpent.

Maybe bigger.

And a damn powerful serpent monster.

Yet that face ... a beautiful heart of a face with huge bright green eyes, and her nose was a button of an upright piglet nose. Those ears, wow, were they **huge**. And they were piggy style too, but those lush juicy lips were pouting cherry sour stern.

Gulp.

(Again?)

Strapped to her lopsided belt of cherry red leather were several pairs of wicked bone stilettos, and a quiver stuffed full of vulture-feathered purple arrows, while in her slim delicate-looking hands, was a spiky and wicked looking dark violet bow made ... from what looked like a wicked a pair of skull and bone scimitars.

No.

Not just looked. It was a sword bow. A pair of swords that could come together into a bow. The quiver wasn't necessary. Not at all. That bow could fire magical bolts of some sort. Maybe more than one kind of magical bolt. The bow's line would be magical too. Strung up magically and automatically.

No need for that quiver and ordinary orc feathers, yet ...

Sinister sexy orcubus girl, and given what she was wearing, and ... no mere fodder orc either.

The card felt like velvet. Its sheen was ... that shine ... foil?

He flipped the card over, but ...

"Stats and name unknown?" Jakon said, "Only says the breed: Orcubus Archer."

More to himself but Ramsel answered anyway.

"Let's see if you have more luck than me," Ramsel said, "Only a truly powerful monster spirit could hope to resist being tamed when forged into a card."

Jakon … hadn't heard of that, but then again, it was so long ago, and he made a point to forget most of what he didn't need to train with.

"We'll see," Jakon said.

"Exactly," Ramsel said.

Holding the card out, Jakon said, "Come forth, minion of my will!"

Nothing happened.

A few young dwarfs gasped. Money got exchanged. While Ramsel chuckled.

"Two more tries," Ramsel said.

Jakon nodded, taking a deep breath. Let his heart thump steady. Like a steam flowing steady.

Breath steady.

"Minion of my will," Jakon said, "Come forth!"

Nothing.

His human side prevented him from forging with these cards but it shouldn't stop him from summoning a monster out of them.

But he wasn't about to show off Azura.

His control of her was … limited, at best, too, but she wasn't averse to listening to him either, probably, as long as he didn't give her orders she disagreed with.

More money exchanged hands between the dwarfs. More than a few discouraged whispers too. Whispers that echoed far too loudly around this round room. While Ramsel grinned a touch too cocky.

"One more try," Ramsel said, "Do not fear failure. No one had yet summoned this lovely orc girl from her card. Not even I. If you do then, I shall acknowledge you as its true wielder."

Jakon grimaced. Even the way Ramsel talked seemed to rub him in the wrong way, but yet, both of them were unable to even summon the monster within it ... maybe this card was defective. It took willpower to control the monster, not to summon it. Letting his dad examine this card ... wait.

A bizarre idea occurred to him, thanks to Gunter.

So Jakon nodded at Ramsel, while grimacing even fiercer at him.

"This card is the rarest of the rare, isn't it?" Jakon said.

"I suspect it," Ramsel said, "But without stats and a name ... orcubus archer cards are on the rare side, but not that rare, since they're only a solid rank or two above orc girl archer."

Ranks and levels and ugh, Jakon didn't remember much of it right now, but time to try something ... unusual, and pleasing to his thumping heart.

Jakon held the card up. Steadied his heart the best he could but ... saying what he planned to out loud ... his cheeks already scolded him plenty, and if it didn't work ...

"Girl of my naughtiest dreams come true!" he said, "Come forth and—"

PUFF!!!!!!

CHAPTER II
FROSTINE

Frostine crouched as small as she could behind the huge jagged boulder. It was shaped like a lopsided chicken egg from some huge chicken, it was half as tall as she was, and lying on its side, yet it was so pale gray it was almost as white as she was.

Almost.

Just the chicken egg appearance ... nonono, her tummy better not growl hungry again.

As the orc deck wielder, she needed to spread half of the orc platoon horde cards close enough to the battlements above.

There were nearly a hundred orc soldiers to a platoon card but each platoon card shouldn't be too close together but not too far apart either–and yet the round bronze gateway that would soon appear and release the orcs ... it would release them several at a time. So it had to remain hidden enough that the orcs wouldn't be mowed down the moment they left the gateways.

She had to crawl here and there without being noticed in the slightest, but the toothy gray walls of the battlements formed the hugest grinning face of the biggest massive dwarf face and more than enough to make her vixen heart run colder than any ... any ... mountain blizzard, yes, mountain blizzard.

She didn't need to glance at the battlements either.

Better not. If she could see it dwarves could see her, and that could spell the end of this invasion, right away.

Her death even.

All their deaths.

She knew the battlements by heart anyway. Knew that wicked evil dwarven grin. It was famous among her kind.

And today, soon, at noon, it would finally be wiped off the face of this world.

CHAPTER 12
SKY

Sky Brewrose savored the sudden, strange rosy fragrance coming off Dirlop Mountain. It was so much like the rose hedges back at home. The hedges she loved wondering in. Getting lost in. They were ever changing. Unlike this mountain of countless never-changing boulders.

Boulders that were so tall and wide she could barely see where she was going. Only she was headed upward. In a very winding, zigzaggy way.

And a glance in the wrong direction ... just how insanely far up she already was. At least a thousand feet. From how that thick canopy below looked more like moss now.

Probably at least a thousand feet.

At least the road itself was chiseled out of the mountain, yet there wasn't a single crack, let alone any potholes—unlike the treacherous road through the forest below. Sigh.

The road even had a sheen. Like the dwarves finished chiseling it just yesterday. Polished it smoother than a fresh rose petal.

Even the wind here was crisp and fresh, unlike that musty forest below. So thick, dark, and so unwelcoming, unlike the forest she called home. Now, up above that canopy, it was finally warm and refreshing again. The sight of the sun too. It blazed well above the forest's canopy.

That Sky was stuck wearing the traditional garb of an elf maiden, a green form-fitting minidress topped with a cowl that seemed to cover more of her than the minidress itself. Her dark green boots were a light leather and low heeled, but with s0lidly gripping soles. Good for climbing trees and walking along branches. Not so much traveling long distance on paved roads. At least strapped to her left thigh was a razor-sharp dagger.

If only she could wear a dress that was long enough to cover the dagger, but no, mom insisted Sky wear traditional elf maiden garb for this journey.

Sigh.

It didn't even match her hair, which was as sky blue as her namesake and waist long, since only low-class elf girls kept their hair shorter than their waist. Still, she managed to sneak in a pink belt and pink fingerless gloves.

Even a pink round cap. A gift from another secret admirer.

An admirer she'd probably never met now, since this journey for training was … going to take a long time.

Too long for any secret admirer to stay an admirer.

But the pink heart bra and panties … a gift from another

admirer she preferred never to meet, but ... sigh, she didn't toss them either. Or burn them, like mom suggested. Or get them cursed, like her friends suggested (as if she could afford that kind of curse. Just because she had some money ...)

But sigh, there was no other chance she'd get another chance to wear anything else except that tradition dark green bra and bottoms—if she hadn't kept the pervy pink gifts.

That they both were very, very visible in this tradition green minidress. All because it had a long wide notch down the torso's middle, and a pair of notches down her hips, with only a few thin but strong strings keeping the minidress snuggly around her hips.

So embarrassing. Why mom insisted on this stretchy suggestive dress, despite it being tradition garb ...

Sigh.

No matter. Every breathe here was like a draught of the best kind of rosehip mead.

If only she didn't run out just as she got here.

(And her vial of healing brew didn't count.)

It was made by her mom. One of the many secret family brews. One her family was especially famous for. So famous her mom hadn't taught her the details of the brew yet. Only bits and pieces. All to ensure it stayed secret.

Of course, that meant Sky had the money for a quality scimitar bow. A bow made of two scimitars that could snap together by their handles. That once snapped together they formed a magical string connecting the blades, and could fire magical bows or, even, regular arrows.

So, of course, her quiver held a full two dozen arrows. The

pine shafts were painted the usual deep green, and feathered with quality cardinal feathers. Even the arrowheads were quality dwarven steel.

And Sky made a point to train as a warrior. To avoid the fate her father suffered at the hands of bandits. Bandits after the recipe of their family's secret brews.

That's why she also made a point to build a resistance to black iron, which normally was searing agony, and which also developed some of her resistance to cold iron. Without that resistance, she'd couldn't even leave the forest she called home. No wood elf was allowed out who didn't have enough resistance to iron. Not when it could be so dangerous, yet so common.

At least the road here was only a few paces wide here, that might of been the reason for so few travelers coming up from this direction. Another reason she chose this way.

There was plenty of room for a slender elf like herself, but barely enough space for any of the stout dwarf merchants that often came to visit her home, let alone the wagons that often came with charging far too loud and fast.

Dirlop Mountain wouldn't have bandits, but Sky didn't care to circle around the Mountain. Spend more time in that thick murky forest more than she needed to. Not with all the tigermite tribes eager to slaughter anyone who came to close to their constantly changing territory.

Not that Sky didn't have confidence in her combat skills, but any sensible warrior avoided unnecessary fights.

Especially with other even more skilled warriors.

Especially such bloodthirsty ones.

But the road going up Dirlop Mountain was very winding and curvy. Maybe she could take a short-cut and try a direct approach. Hopping on the larger taller boulders.

Good training too.

Once she opened her spores, she could walk along vertical surfaces, if not very steep ones, but no. Focus on getting to the back gates before lunchtime. Or else she might have to wait outside for hours until the guards returned.

If what her mom had warned her about was true.

And judging by the sun ... it was too close to noon for comfort.

Time for a short—the smell of fox?

A sinister giggle?

"Zee dwarves shall never know what hit them."

A girls' voice. Behind the sharp curve of the road ahead.

"Pearl. Take care not to be too loud." a gruff guy said, "A stray dwarf—"

"Will die by my hand," Pearl said, "Just like the last four. Jaydorn and Gron. Ensure there's no one coming this way. If there is ... kill them quick and painfully—he-he."

Sky gulped. Bandits? She had to warn the dwarves inside.

Not pick fight she might lose. Not so close to her destination.

Time for a short cut.

Sky style.

So she dashed off the road. Far off the road.

Then with some luck she found a way to hop on top of the boulders. Up and up and up.

And wow, was this place like a forest of jagged boulders.

If it weren't for the incline, she'd have no idea which direction to head in.

So squatting low Sky hopped up the slope.

When Sky heard another sinister giggle.

A few boulders ahead of her.

And below.

CHAPTER 13
JAKON

Jakon thought his heart stopped for a moment.

No.

More than a moment.

Several moments. Well beyond ... well ...

The card in his hand was gone.

Before him was a puff of bright red smoke, as large, no, a bit larger than he was. Taller and wider, like a bubbly boulder of smoke. And the smell, it was ... cherry musk? Yeah.

It was so much like what he read elf girls should smell like, well, if they don't wash enough, they smelled fruity and that muskiness, like a feminine version of what that elf boy Ramsel smelled like.

The puff of smoke was billowing out and circling around just like a proper monster card summoning. He'd seen this hundreds, no, thousands of times, back as a little dwarf with Gunter, and his heart raced so quick, so amazed and ... even just a while ago, with his other card, the new one with the crisis snake orc thing.

(Never mind Azura and her ... antics.)

His boots were solid on the stone floor. He was steady, in his slacks and jerkin, yet that cherry sweet musk, no, the round room was so silent, and not from the padded walls.

All the dwarfs were so shocked they couldn't even gasp. Yank their beards. Even if they were young dwarfs, so their beards only came down to their waists and were right by their thick hands.

There weren't even any coins clinging.

(Yet.)

But by ... by Gelgorn's Hammer! Jakon could barely gasp. Just like many of the young chubby dwarves.

The orcubus archer girl was ... only a pace away and she was ... was ... as drop dead deadly gorgeous as her illustration and very much right in front of him, and so, so close, he could feel her warm cheery breath and it was crazy fresh and refreshing.

She even giving him an intensely cherry sour pour. Her wicked sword bow pointed down, to the side, yet clearly ready in her slim hands to feather down anything in less than an instant.

Her cowled bra top and short-short skirt of bright violet and very form-fitting scales ... curved slim in the right places, obese in the chest places was right. Her top barely fit that chest, and his stupid cheeks were blazing hotter, had to be even redder than her bright red and beautiful skin.

Her cherry musk was just the topping of the cherry dessert she was to the eyes and loins.

"Master Ogle," she said, and flicked her long beautiful cherry hair to the side. Sending him another breeze of her cherry sweet musk.

She even gave him another sly knowing smirk. Even with the silence. So deafening.

Except for the thunk thunk thunk of his own heart.

"I ... I ..." Jakon said, and finally, he gulped. Loud and clear.

Too clear. Loud.

Who would be the master and ... and ... gulp.

"Orders?" she said, and so sultry suggestive even the oldest of the dwarves here blushed redder than her skin.

Even Ramsel did. Enough to almost hide his utter shock.

Almost.

His swords were still out and floating around him.

"Um ..." Jakon said, "Ah, name?"

"Sure," the orcubus archer said, "You may name me. Please grant me a name as cute as me, hmmm?"

Wha ... she didn't ... or she did, and preferred a new name?

"You ... don't have a name?" he said.

"Master Perv," she said, "You may name me *what**ever** you like."

Uh huh ... she even huffed that obese chest of her out toward him. Her breath. So cherry warm and fresh. Her beauty ...

Gulp.

"Do you …" he said, "Wish to be free? As a living monster card you … well … a dwarf …"

"Oh, I know," she said, "But no. I choose to go living monster card. Quite a while ago, in fact, if you catch me drift, hmmmm?"

Jakon nodded. "Immorality, beauty, and power all at the cost of your freedom, ey? Well, until you're killed in deck combat, or worse."

"No one is truly free," she said, and smirked far too knowingly, "Your dwarven … morals are restrictions you choose to live by, hmmm? And life can do worse without deck battles. At least as a living monster card, I … ah, you truly don't realize *that* yet, hmmm?"

"That?" Jakon said.

"Oh," she said, "I won't spoil the surprise. Enjoy me serving and pleasuring you, please, alright?"

That smirk of hers … Jakon … he knew better than to take this all at face value yet …

"Alright," he said, "But if any of my orders are too … unpleasant then–"

"No matter," she said, "Orders are orders, and the perks of going living card monster, come with a price, yes?"

"But some prices …" Jakon said, and grimaced.

"Risk and reward," she said, "If you aren't pleased with me, then return me to the boy who gifted me to you. I don't mind. But I'll only serve who I choose, and how. Living monster cards aren't exactly slaves, unless … you have a compulsion complex card?"

The way she raised her black eyebrow ... so calm yet all too attentively ...

"No," Jakon said, "I don't think ..."

"Too bad," she said, "Making you waste one ..."

Her smirk. Okay. She was enjoying this far more than he himself ever could in her situation.

But ... something was off. Azura too. Both girls were far too confident, too sexually suggestive despite their comprised situation, unless ...

"Fine," Jakon said, "To each their own, Scarlet Death."

That name got him nice happy smirk from her. It was from a heroine from those dime dreadfuls. One of the ancient Seven Deadly Serpents, actually, even if technically, that one wasn't a serpent but a scarlet vixen beast elf, who burned her serpent masters all too avenge her clan.

"Ooo, nice name," she said, "Thanks. I'll be sure to be their deaths. Your enemies, that is."

The orcubus archer even giggled sultry nice.

"In return for such a nice name," she said, "I'll give you a warning. My precious master ... isn't as nice as he seems."

Ramsel grimaced, but said nothing. He simply waited a few paces behind Scarlet. The whole time. He hadn't even ogled her. Not once. Just a look full of scorn, but orcs and elves never got along well, so having an orc living card monster ... sigh.

Jakon scratched his beard stubble. "I appreciate the warning," he said, "but I'll make my own decision about him."

Scarlet chuckled. Nodded.

"Card time?" she said, and slumped slightly, and very cutesy sultry.

"Exactly," Jakon said, nodding, and–

PUFF!!!!

Scarlet puffed into a cherry cloud? He didn't even ... sigh. She must really have far more freedom that she let on. Azura too.

It was better that way, probably, but Jakon hoped he'd learn just how much, since both of them were darklings that ... no, betraying their deck master ... no. Some restrictions ... no, just no.

She returned to her velvety foil card in his hand, and he slipped her into his dozen card deck.

Well, baker's dozen now.

Ramsel was clearly holding back a scowl, so Jakon gave him a respectful curtsy.

"Thank you for helping my classmates," Jakon said, "and for this orcubus archer card. I'll cherish her greatly."

Ramsel returned the curtsy, but his swords vanished. Finally.

"Maybe another time ... Jakon, is it?" Ramsel said.

"Yes, I'm Jakon. Ramsel, I hope to see you again."

"Pity you arrived too late," Ramsel said, "Maybe after lunch I shall return and spar with you, but for now, I must fulfill the rest of my duties. I take my leave."

"So formal," Jakon said, "So thank you again."

And Jakon bowed deeper this time. Very formally too.

A final curtsy and Ramsel was off.

Yet Jakon, his stomach ... even more uneasy now.

CHAPTER 14
RAMSEL

Ramsel quietly cursed his luck, but he had accomplished most of what he needed to do at the blademaster academy. The scentless poison coating his steel sabers should start weakening the dwarf students soon enough.

All except that Jakon.

Maybe.

But as a beast elf, even in wood elf form, the poison wouldn't affect him in the slightest. Not without s solid scratch from the blades.

A scratch none of those dwarfs would be strong enough to inflict on him. Not ever again.

Soon the countless gemstones throughout the ceiling would soon belong to his kind. Wealth that would buy the freedom of his clan from the lower slave ranks. His ample skill in bladework was the only reason he was granted such a coveted position beside such a precious vixen like Frostine.

His thin leather boots didn't make a sound against the granite floor. He was more than silent enough for his next task. A task connected to Frostine being more clever than she let on. Letting that tigermite elder send one of their better warrior females to seek out another attack route, as if Frostine would humor any of their warriors escaping the carding they were destined for.

All he needed to do was follow the faintly glowing outline of an orange cat girl swimming through what seemed solid rock, but what, he already knew now was another secret passageway in and out of Dirlop Mountain.

A passageway Frostine had prepared him to use—to escape.

After he carded that tigermite girl.

The tunnel opened up into a huge cavern. With walled craters full of beautifully blue water. Crates that ceiling spikes were dripping water into. Drip drip drip.

Like blood from a freshly hanging corpse.

Right now there were too many dwarfs. All shopping and going about their daily business. For now.

Once the attack began, once the dwarves fled, he could finish his task here.

Summon the handful of tigermite warriors, all from living monster cards. Frostine granted him the temporary boost in magical power needed for it.

That she'd trust a lowly dog like him, he wouldn't let her down.

He would die before failing.

But losing that orcubus archer ... despite his ... difficulty in summoning her ... Frostine would not be happy. The orcubus archer could of been used for alchemy parts, if nothing else, especially since she wasn't undead like the other orcs in Frostine's monster card deck.

But no matter.

The tigermite girl was getting closer and closer, and Ramsel quietly headed over to the crater she'd headed toward, no doubt would surface in. Try to remain hidden until the preordained attack.

But going back through the route—not possible for her.

Not with the spell his next card casted on the surface of the crater's water. She couldn't wield any magical techniques —until she was properly carded, as she should of been weeks ago.

Soon she'd replace that treacherous orcubus archer, whether as a warrior, or just for alchemy parts, she'd play her role in the downfall of Dirlop Mountain.

Whether she wanted to, or not.

CHAPTER 15
JAKON

His stomach still remained uneasy by the time Jakon got back to his familiar anvil of a kitchen at home. The sleek stone walls sheened with the usual diamonds. The gemstones all glowed high in the ceiling. Hmmm.

Wait.

That elf guy hadn't commented at all on the gemstones. Strange. Humans usually did. Eyed them wide and greedy, more often than not. Why so many other races treated gemstones like currency rather than the practical materials they were ...

Wait.

Ah!

The smell of lunch hit his nose like a troll's club to the nose, but in the best way possible. It wiped away that uneasy like ... like ... wow.

Gone.

(Mostly.)

Right on the black rose table. Before each rose-themed chair. On a that special set of plates made of rings of black roses tight together, lunch was … wow.

There it was.

Outright mountain high hordes of sliced thick and gooey corned beef, and the corned beef was of the fattiest and greasiest kind.

On each of the three plates the mountain of corned beef was stuffed ultra-thick between two superthick and amazingly soft slices of seeded rye bread.

A real dwarf's lunch.

One of the best too. And the reason why mom hadn't shown up to the blademaster academy today.

Even the air here was hotter than usual. Hot and humid. Enough to make Jakon breath a bit harder. As if he went through some serious training. Simply from standing here.

But that was from the combination of the smithy and the massive amount of cooking going on below. The vents below were a bit too close to the vents to these rooms so they always got a good bit warmer, and that was intentional.

It was a reliable way to ensure the dwarves here could feel the familiar warmth of the smithy below.

A smithy Jakon made a point not to visit too much of anymore … but …

"Oh Jakon! Sit down! Eat eat!" mom said, but from behind Jakon?

Sigh, a good reminder how must more skilled she was, sneaking up behind him so easily ...

"Okay ..." he said and sat down at his usual seat, the newest chair, and ... actually, his plate had the highest mountain of corned beef and thickest slices of rye bread.

As nice as this all was ... it was too nice.

His dad marched into the room, in his usual thick gray smithery apron on and long flowing beard of trim black over it.

"Ah, there you are, good," his dad said, and heaved something over his shoulder. Something long, about half Jakon's own height, and it was wrapped in a thick white blanket?

His dad marched right over to his own chair. Settled the long, blanket-wrapped something against his chair. And sat down with a hurrumpf.

A very fine and ... happy sounding hurrumpf?

Hmmm.

Jakon went over to his seat and sat down, but didn't eat. Yet.

Mom already took her own seat. "Father has good news for you."

"Excellent news," dad said, "A true dwarf does trust his eyes, and more than a few dwarves up in the battlements saw that castle of yours."

Jakon nodded. Smiled. Despite the warmth of being acknowledged, what that castle could actually mean ... it iced his spine too, but he knew better than to say anything.

Yet.

His dad went on.

"With the increase in tigermite sightings," dad said, "And orcs here and there, there's no chance of you heading anywhere anytime soon. No one's being let out, except those who know how to defend themselves real well from the usual trouble. So no more worries about leaving anytime soon, that is."

Mom … didn't look as happy as dad, but nodded.

"A scouting party was sent out," mom said, "To check on–"

"No need to worry our boy," dad said, "Those companions of his, well, I'm sure they'll arrive safe and sound. Tunker's leading the scouting party and nothing get passed Tunker."

That perked Jakon up. "Tunker? Then …"

Mom tsked. "And you asked me not to worry him, when you went ahead and did it anyway."

"I …" dad said, "Well, you're right when you right, but the boy already knew he had companions coming. But enough about that. I've got something good to give him. Something better than any of those spores and whatnot."

Dad patted that thing wrapped up in a blanket.

Then he whipped it off.

Revealing a short broadsword, with a thick triangular blade, the … shining steel(?) blade was as pale blue as the clearest sky, so clearly a very special blade. The hilt was a deep but bright lighting blue. Solid and scaled like an overgrown serpent, and it was shaped like a cross between a wicked tulip and a cyclopic dragon head, but the polished round gemstone was a pale empty blue. The handle was like a spiraled dragon tail, and looked incredibly solid and a good grip.

"That's …" Jakon said.

"A serpent slayer blade," dad said, "Forged from a truly powerful dragon of ancient times. Its power … amazing, but no need to worry about spores to use this fellow. It can do plenty … once it accepts you."

"Accepts me?" Jakon said.

Mom sighed, and frowned so deep …

"It's a magical blade," she said, "A living blade. Your stamina is enough–as long as it accepts you as its wielder. A big if, and living blades–"

Dad laughed, but clearly knew better than say anything. Yet.

Mom sighed again. "Just say what you're going to say."

Now dad said it.

"Living blades," dad said, "A step up–no. A **few** good steps above those monster cards you loved as a kid—and, I'm proud to see, you're finally getting into again. With living monster cards … troublesome, but winning one over … few can do it right, and you did, from what I heard, and building a whole deck of living monster cards, the right way, they can protect you like loyal personal guards, if, well, anyway, you're old enough to know to do the right thing. Now where was I …"

Dad hoisted the blade. Patted proudly.

"Ah yes," dad said, "Living blades are made from living monster cards. The right ones. And this blade, long ago, was made from the best. Come and take it. Give it a try."

Great! Jakon stood up and reached for the sword when— ack!

BOOM!!!

CHAPTER 16
JAKON

A boom rumbled the whole anvil of a kitchen? A boom from a distance? A good solid distance. Enough to wobble Jakon in his place as he stood by the heavy iron table and chair. His corned beef sandwich wobbled almost as much as him, but fell apart even quicker.

That the boom's rumble was so intense, it forced him to catch the heavy table to steady himself. Yet the table itself shook. Shook enough that it was hard to hold it.

The smell of broken rock filled the room. A smell far too familiar from the mines. From exploring the deepest mines far back in his younger days.

A gust of air? Far too fresh and cool. Outside air.

As if a massive window was opened nearby.

What was going on? Jakon had somehow already grabbed that stunningly gorgeous serpent slaying short sword. Its eyes were blank, as if as shocked as mom and dad. They both held the table, struggling too, their sandwiches becoming as ruined as his own.

Screams erupted.

Squeals.

Orc squeals!

Jakon gasped. "Attack! We're under attack!"

And he dashed out. Toward the source of fresh air.

Before mom or dad could stop him.

Through the hallway with the paintings of his ancestors.

Ancestor who must of been as shocked as he was.

At the gap that once was his bedroom wall. Now a wide view. A craggy cliff. Shattered rocks.

And countless orc warriors charging upwards.

CHAPTER 17
SKY

Sky crouched as close to the tall jagged boulder as she could dare. The surface of the rock here looked as sharp as the dagger strapped to her thigh. Mom had warned her about how sharp some of the boulders in back of Dirlop Mountain were.

Warned her not to go off the road.

But no. Sky risked it. Better some sharp rocks than some bandits ready for a fight.

Or so she thought.

A boom rumbled nearby. Enough to shake the very mountain itself. Like thunder, but the sky was as clear and blue as her hair.

And the wind carried the smell of chalk? Like the classroom back when she was far younger. A classroom she did her best not to fall asleep in too often, but failed at that a bit too much, until Teacher learned she was allergic to clouds of chalk and used them to make her sneeze awake.

Her nose was already itching to sneeze.

But the smell of fox below? Another sinister giggle.

And her hackles tingled harshly. Just like whenever she entered the local hedgewitch's shop back at home.

A witch bandit?

Sky already had her two scimitars in hand. All her training was meant for a moment like this. Not to run. But to find a way to escape. Survive. Fight the bandits only if necessary.

Especially if one of them was a witch.

Maybe even a vixen witch.

Best retreat for now. The witch clearly sensed Sky was nearby. She'd be ready for any ambush. Just like how the hedgewitch back at home could always sense Sky's presence —or absence.

She turned. And—ack!

Behind the boulder beside her. A shadow of a man. With a long foxy snout and foxy ears.

A fox beast man.

An enemy.

With a pair of short swords.

Sky drew an arrow. A regular arrow. Less noisy than her magical ones.

He slipped beyond the boulder. And spotted her.

Just as she fired. Her arrow plunged deep into his eye.

He gasped. Trembled.

Her next arrow plunged into his bare chest. Felling him.

That's when countless squeals of bloodthirsty orcs roared from down the mountain. From among the boulders.

Sky turned toward the orcs and—ack!

A shadow over her. Another fox man! Lunging for her. From behind.

She spun around.

Clang!

Her scimitar bow deflected—black iron claw extenders? Just a single scratch would be agony! Maybe even poison her —if it was cold iron, not just black iron.

His wiry weight pressed her down. His strength well beyond her own.

That he only wore filthy slacks ...

Bad enough that his rancid breath even weakened her gut, but her combat instructor was just as gross at times too.

And taught her what to do.

(Or close enough ... hopefully.)

She leapt backwards. Falling. Only instants to react.

The fox man growled down at her. But also shocked.

Unbalanced.

While Sky already had another arrow strung.

When the top of the boulder exploded! From pink lightning?!

Vaporizing everything. Including the fox man.

An instant later, a white fox girl in snake-bone armor appeared on top of the rock. Her long hair was as strangely pink as her lightning. Just as pink as her claw extenders.

The fox girl smirked. "One less elf girl."

"One less vixen," Sky said, and loosed the arrow.

The fox girl looked down. Shocked.

Just as Sky smashed into the ground. Stars spinning throughout her sight.

And the fox girl deflected the arrow with her claw extenders.

But not the magical bolt that followed it.

An amber sunfire energy. It bolt exploded the moment it touched those claw extenders.

BOOM!

The rumble ... not her magical bolt but ... her head. Her mom warned her not to use the magical bolts yet. Her spores were needed. Or else ... else ... ugh. The squeals of blood thirsty orcs were getting closer and closer and—

Huh?

The fox girl was back. On top of the rock. But without any armor. Or claw extenders.

Bare in the fur, the fox girl even pouted sour down at Sky. Looming over her. Even licked her chops. Like Sky was a tasty treat to be.

"Such powerful magic, no?" the fox girl said, "Too bad. Your turn to—"

Sky ripped her dagger out. Flung it up so quick.

The fox girl flung her hands out. Pink lightning coming.

Caught the dagger. Exploding it. The shard ripping into the fox girl. Making her yowl.

Giving Sky another chance.

A chance she didn't waste.

The next arrow plunged right into the fox girl's chest. Through her evil heart.

"No ..." the fox girl said, "I ... the orcs ... not. *yet.*"

Sky fired another arrow. Right through the vixen's eye. Into her brain.

Sky rolled to the side. Just as the vixen crashed into the ground.

And the squeals of orcs vanished?

Except for a bunch of distance squeals. From the other side of the mountain.

Sky trembled. Braced herself.

She trained to fight. Defended herself. And even Dirlop Mountain.

Time to prove herself again.

CHAPTER 18
JAKON

OOM!

From nearby. The smell of more shattered rocks. A cloud of gray fumed from the wall. More orcish squeals of bloodthirsty glee.

Yet Jakon held himself back from lunging off the ledge. For a moment. Access the situation for a moment.

Just a moment.

The air itself. The stink of orc. And worse. Of the awful burnt death he read about countless times in his dime dreadfuls.

His heart raged. His grip on the magical short sword got tighter and tighter. The damage from the attack was clear.

Below him the craggy jagged incline was too steep to charge down.

Too new. Too jagged.

Too many warthog-faced orcs screaming. Their iron scimitars waving for dwarf blood.

And not enough dwarven axes waving back.

Yet.

Too many enemies to climb down the slope carefully.

Another bolt of blue lightning? Striking nearby. Another wall.

Another boom.

More shattered rock. More dust biting his breathe. A gray cloud fuming. Hiding more death and destruction.

When a bolt of blue lightning struck at him.

Struck the sword.

And got sucked in? Absorbed!

Powered him up stronger than any of mom's corned beef sandwiches could. Jakon roared with dwarven fury. Bellowed with dwarven rage.

And leapt. Down the steep jagged slope. Jumping down boulder after boulder.

Into the midst of the orcs.

Cutting them down. His blade slicing quickly. Deadly.

And through their leather tunics with ease. Smashing through the wooden shields were less ease. Shattering their iron blades with only a little more effort.

A dance to the deadly doom.

Another bolt came his way.

Almost zipped above him.

But forks down. Struck his sword instead?

Got absorbed again!

And now even the orc's iron shields posed no barrier to his blade. Nothing stopped his dance of orc death.

Except for the orc numbers.

More and more and more.

When he spotted the source of the lightning—a snow vixen witch.

Like an evil Azura.

On top of a ring of tall craggy boulders. A dozen paces away. Downwards.

The snow vixen looked right up at him. In snake-themed bone armor and snarling vicious.

Good. Time to end this attack. Now.

CHAPTER 19
JAKON

Jakon bellowed again. Roaring louder than any boom from a lightning bolt. Roaring louder than any smithy hammer. Than any fire raging above.

Charged faster than any arrow. Faster than any lesser blade.

The boulders were there to be hopped across. The wide winding trails around them thick with orcs.

Orcs dying by his blade.

But with more and more replaced them. Their piggish sty stink curling his gut. His rage too great to make any comment. Or quip.

Only bellow some more.

But the orcs scattered? Charging past him? Under him.

Trying to avoid him?!

He cut down as many as he could. But ... wait. Bronze ring gateways? Hidden by some of the larger craggier boulders ahead. Jakon leapt passed them. Behind the bronze rings were empty. Just turning round and round as they floated.

Until Jakon slashed one. Destroying it quickly.

And then another.

And another.

PUFF!

PUFF!

PUFF!

Cards? Destroyed cards. Screamed from above. Orcish screams of death.

Perfect!

Destroyed the rings and kill the orcs.

But the rings were stashed between boulders. Hard to find from the ground. From the same level.

But Jakon as a dwarf. He wasn't about to give up so quickly.

When a wiry fox man suddenly slashed at Jakon. From behind another boulder!

Long black claw extenders slashed at his throat.

Clang.

Clang.

Clang.

Blade against blade. Training saved Jakon. No need to think.

Only act.

Yet the fox warrior pressed him back. The furball was only in slacks. No doubt relying on his regeneration rather than armor.

And a fatal mistake. Once Jakon managed to cut through his defenses.

As long as no orcs came to the fox's aid.

And—

A purple blur zipped passed Jakon's head.

And a purple arrow sprouted from the fox warrior's eye. The smell of cherry musk behind Jakon ...

"Scarlet?" Jakon said.

"Can't let my master be outdone by some wretched fox boy," Scarlet said.

The fox warrior snarled. "Traitor! Ramsel will avenge me."

"Ramsel ..." Jakon said, his heart sinking terrified of what he'd find when he got back ...

And the fires of vengeance burning even hotter.

Almost as hot as the ball of flame—ball of flame!

From his left!

Jakon leapt back. Tried something desperate.

He leapt at the flame. Swung his sword at it.

Absorbed it.

Just the fox warrior lunged at him. About to slice his throat.

But another arrow sprouted from his chest. And he gurgled. And collapsed. Shoving the arrow through even more.

"Scarlet ..." Jakon said.

"Thank me later," Scarlet said, "with your dick."

"I ..." Jakon said, his cheeks burning hotter than ... than ...

Gulp.

Scarlet let out a laugh. "Don't overthink it. Crude humor is part of the battle field, my little virgin sweet—"

A cry rang out to his left. A scarlet fox girl. Small chested and in a black cowled bra top and skirt.

Not armor.

No claw extenders either.

Yet she snarled. "How dare you! Die! Die with Drano!"

And blasted more fireballs at him.

But Jakon charged at her. His blade absorbed each and every fireball.

Her gasp. Her last.

His blade plunged right through her chest. Through her heart.

"No ..." she said, "I don't ... not here ... *please.*"

How many dwarves didn't get the chance to ask for mercy.

As if any would.

"Yes. *here,*" Jakon said and kicked her off his blade.

She smashed into a boulder behind her. Collapsed. Dying on the ground. From his dime dreadfuls he knew her end would come soon enough. But her regeneration would keep her alive for a while longer.

But only a little.

When Scarlet screamed. "Your right!"

CHAPTER 20
RAMSEL

Ramsel cursed his luck thrice, and once again.

The expected booms had rumbled the whole mountain, as they should, since both Frostine and Pearl were skilled vixen witches. Their lightning potent—when used right.

Even the smell of shattered rock fumed through the cavern. Biting his breathe harsh, but not as harsh had he been in his beast form rather than his wood elf form.

It tinged the air everywhere a dark gray. Clouding the light from the precious gemstones lining the ceiling. Blocking his sight of the other craters.

But not the one in front of him.

Giving Ramsel more leeway to act. The gasps of shock and dismay were nothing compared to what was coming.

The ceiling spikes shook like shivering dogs. Splattering

water everywhere. A few even fell. Shattering against the floor.

But also shocking the dwarves into action.

The clonk of their iron boots as they dashed toward the rumbles. The booms.

And now, the squeal of undead orcs yearning for blood-thirsty vengeance.

But no matter. The orange outline of the tigermite girl, his final target was getting closer and closer to the crater he was in front of. The spikes and wall around it, the slits in the wall weren't too thin for him to slip through.

Or his many blades.

The cries of shock. Alarm.

The dwarves finally realized they were under attack. Shouts for arms. To be ready for battle.

A battle a few of the closest dwarves never saw before Ramsel summoned his many steel sabers, before he slaughtered them, unseen, and unexpected.

More than enough time to summon his carded tigermite warriors. A dozen of their best from the forest below. All guys, of course, as Frostine chuckled to him, as if she knew he preferred men over women. Maybe she did. She was more clever than she let on.

Not the tigermites had their katars ready. They dashed away killing the unarmed, unexpecting dwarfs. Helping remove the "dwarven eyesore" from their beloved land.

When a cry rang out—and not a dwarven one.

Another yowl?

And another?

Ramsel snarled. "Who dares—"

Two more yowls. His tigermites were being slain? By who?

Their katars were covered with Crippling dwarven poison. A single scratch would do a dwarf in. Just the smell would weaken them. And it was scentless. So with the gray clouding the air, the dwarves would never notice until it was too late.

Yet yowl after yowl after yowl and …

"So you're the one who harmed my students."

Behind him?

A human woman? Thin. Scrawny. In a pathetic tattered dress.

And only one saber in her hand? Ha!

No need to hid his true nature any longer.

Ramsel transformed into his fox warrior form. Drew out all his sabers.

All hundred of them.

And yet they shattered before he knew it. His chest. Blood. Darkness.

Impossible. How could he fail here? When he was so close …

"My hundred …" he said, "how could one …"

"Blademaster secret," the women said, "You had some promise, had you not crippled so many of my students …"

A splash. Behind him.

"Master?!" Ivy said, "Wha … oh no."

The woman chuckled? "No need to sneak about anymore."

"Oh ..." Icy said, "Then ... I'm captured?"

The splash of cat girl leaving the crater water.

Stepping closer.

And closer.

The darkness growing darker.

And darker.

The woman sighed. "Behave yourself, and I'll make sure you'll be fine."

"Ooo," Ivy said, "Okay!"

And that sleeved paw of Ivy in sight. Right by him.

And a card dagger in his hand ...

Pain? He yowled.

Hacked up blood.

"Careful Ivy," the woman said, "You almost got carded."

"Ooo," Ivy said, "I recognize him. He's ..."

But Ramsel knew no more.

CHAPTER 21
JAKON

The moment Scarlet screamed Jakon turned right.

Just in time.

Toward a scarlet and black blur. One lunging from behind another craggy boulder. His heart jumped even faster. His neck and chest so bare.

Despite his jerkin. It wasn't armor. Not by far.

Too much like another ambush by his mom.

One he'd learned to survive.

Almost.

Jakon didn't stumble back. That wouldn't give him time.

Not without throwing off his balance.

Time slowed down. Drastically.

The small-chested scarlet fox was crumbled and dying by one boulder beside Jakon. Her gasps and moans only roiled his blood more.

No dodging to that side.

The fox warrior was dead a couple paces to his other side. No dodging in that direction either.

Time for another death.

Another scarlet fox girl. A truly busty beautiful one. Even when she was snarling. Lunging at him.

With fiery claw extenders. Slashing toward his neck.

Behind her several paces of space. For her to retreat. If needed. No. *When* needed. Before a large craggy boulder.

No. A wall of boulders.

Jakon stepped back. Carefully. Slowly. His speed. So slow.

But training made him fast enough.

Just enough.

And clang!

Blocked her slash.

Absorbing some of the flames. Giving him another much-needed boost. Speeding up time. But only for him.

Clang.

Clang.

Clang.

More strikes. More blocks. Less and less flame on her claws. More absorbed by his sword.

His heart thumped even harder each and every time. His breathe even more strained. Like his body was being forged by the sword itself. Each time it absorbed more magic.

The busty fox girl was pushing him back. More and more.

Her claws getting closer and closer to his neck. His chest.

He needed to turn this around.

And quickly.

Time to pull a trick from his dime dreadfuls.

"You're almost too sexy to slay," Jakon said, "Almost."

The busty fox girl leapt back, and huffed, but with a pleased smirk?

"Right back at you," the busty fox girl said, but how much she meant it ... even a breeze of her fox scent wasn't that bad.

If she hadn't helped attack his home ...

A purple flash. Right by his head.

Zipped to the fox girl's big lovely green eye. Enough to ache his heart stupid when—

Clang.

Deflected?

"Nice try," the busty fox girl said, "Ruby Ripclaw."

"I'm Scarlet now. Scarlet Death. *Your* death."

"Whatever," the busty fox girl said, "I'm Saphira Sultry-tail. You?"

"Jakon Dawdora."

"Dawdora ..." Saphira said, and snarled. "My sisters! Your clan used them as materials and—"

"No! No! No!" a pair of girls said, from his card deck?

Saphira gasped. "Impossible they ..."

An arrow sprouted from her chest. She gasped.

"Damn you, Ruby," Saphira said, her knees trembling but ... oh crap.

She yanked the arrow from her chest. Only a little blood was on the tip.

Her breasts actually caught it? Protected her?

She even smirked. "Another perk of having big breasts."

Clang!

Saphira deflected another arrow from Scarlet.

"Scarlet!" Jakon said, "Wait a moment. Saphira, let me card you. Then you and your sisters—"

"Give me back my sisters," Saphira said, "and ... no. The Dragon Lords would slay us all, my whole clan, if I surrendered so easily. ... sorry Jakon. I—"

"Understand," he said, and lunged.

Full power. His breathe had returned. His power. Even stronger.

Her claw extenders clashed. Tried to catch his blade. Deflect it.

But shattered?

Her shock. Almost as great as his own.

His blade plunged right through her chest. Her big breasts no protection this time.

She coughed up blood.

"Don't resist the carding," he said, and slipped out an empty card.

She grimaced. "I won't. You win."

The card transformed into a dagger. A dagger he plunged into her.

The next moment— PUFF! A scarlet cloud of smoke. Smelling of her gentle fox scent. Then she was gone. Now one of his new monster cards.

A card he quickly slipped back into his deck.

Scarlet tsked. "Carding every big breasted beauty now?"

"Scarlet, I ..." Jakon said.

"Snag this last vixen without me then," Scarlet said.

Oh no—PUFF!

CHAPTER 22
JAKON

That cloud of cherry musk swirling toward Jakon. Only paces away. From on top of a low boulder. Where Scarlet had been.

Scarlet went back to her card form. And into his deck?

By herself?

His breathe was ragged but still steady. His strength still there. Like dwarven steel. It wouldn't give in. He wouldn't shatter like less human steel. Not until the job was done and his home safe again.

But now for the final enemy.

The snow vixen in snake-bone armor loomed over him. On top of a ring of tall boulders. She glared down at him.

Her bone claw extender crackled with blue lightning.

Yet ... she really did look too much like Azura—except for the color of her long blonde hair.

"I see," the snow vixen said, "Zhat blade is troublesome.

But I'll spare your measly life if you let me card Rubica and give me back Saphira. A good deal, no?"

That first scarlet fox girl must of been Rubica.

"So the fox guy ..." Jakon said.

"Already dead," the snow vixen said, "so he cannot be carded, no?"

True. Good. He didn't want to spare any of them. Saphira just got lucky by having sisters he already carded. More like received as cards.

"Call off the orcs too," Jakon said, "and I'll consider it ... Ms ..."

"Frostine," she said, "but zee orcs cannot be recalled. They seek vengeance for their deaths and vill fight until no dwarves remain—or they themselves die again."

Jakon huffed, and glared back at Frostine. Either she was a necromancer or a monster card deck wielder. Either way defeating her should end the orc menace too.

"I'll let you card Rubica," he said, "but when I defeat you, you let me card you too—and keep Rubica as well."

That got him a very sour grimace back. But vixen witch cards were valuable. Especially living ones.

"*When?*" Frostine said, "Big talk for a little dwarf, no?"

"Big request for a little furball," Jakon said.

"Ooo," Frostine said, "Not fleabag? Interesting. Fine, I accept your terms—as long as when I defeat you, you accept my request."

"Request?" he said, "What?"

"You'll see," she said, "Soon enough, no?"

Jakon almost pressed her, but no. She'd refuse, and maybe refuse to come closer.

Getting her down from on top of the boulder was the first priority. Getting her within reach of his blade. And with honorable dwarven means.

That meant letting her to card that first scarlet fox girl Rubica before she finished dying.

"Alright," Jakon said, and backed away from the small-chest fox girl.

Frostine hopped down. Landed right beside Rubica.

"You vill not strike me while I card her?" Frostine said, and she even already had another empty card out. A card she transformed into a dagger.

"Of course not," Jakon said, "A deal is a deal."

"Zhen lower your blade," Frostine said.

"Dwarf's honor," Jakon said, "I—"

"But half dwarf," Frostine said, "means half the honor, no?"

That got a snarl from Jakon.

"*No,* a dwarf is a dwarf," Jakon said, "Card Rubica now, or let her die. Your choice, Frostine. I won't attack until you're done and ready."

Frostine let out what sounded like ... a la-sigh?

"Fine," Frostine said, "When I card you, I vill expect much."

"Right back at you," Jakon said.

Frostine la-sighed again. While facing him, she slipped beside Rubica and, right as Rubica gurgled a wait, Frostine stabbed her.

"Zorry, Rubica," Frostine said, "Vee serve in life and death, no?"

Rubica gasped, nodded, and exploded into a scarlet cloud of smoke and transformed into a card, which Frostine slipped into a deck ... between her big breasts.

Jakon growled. "Ready?"

"Almost," Frostine said, "Zee carding is almost ... saddening, no?"

"Enough chit chat," Jakon said, "Time to die."

"But I am not ready," Frostine said, "and you promised to vait until I vas, no?"

"I ..." Jakon said, gnashed his teeth, and nodded. "Hurry up."

"Give me a few moments," Frostine said, and took a deep breath, "Such a fierce dwarf boy. Fighting you is so thrilling. I must calm myself."

Uh huh. She meant recover some strength.

"I didn't say you could rest up before our fight," Jakon said.

"You never said I couldn't," Frostine said, "In fact, on your honor, I might as vell recover. It looks like you could use a rest too, no?"

"My home—" Jakon said.

"No different than mine," Frostine said, "after you dwarves raided it. Took my cute little sister. If it were not for my beloved Dragon Lord I vould of shared zee same fate."

"A dragon that—" Jakon said,

When a fierce overwhelming roar came from on top of the mountain.

CHAPTER 23
JAKON

Jakon barely managed not to gasp. That roar shook everything. Even the whole mountain. To the very core.

Just the wind, it carried the stink of serpent now. Enough to sour his appetite. Even for mom's coming corned beef sandwiches. Fresh or reheated.

No doubt the delicious reward for defending Dirlop Mountain.

Because curled on the top spire of a peak … a scarlet dragon. Several times bigger than a war stallion. Wings out wide and endless times more fierce than any other beast he ever saw.

A dragon that glared their way.

No.

At Frostine a few paces away from Jakon.

"Master?" Frostine said, and la-sighed again, "Oh vell, vee must fight now. I shall try to card you, instead of outright killing you. Vill you do zee same for me? Please? I am quite worth the carding, no?"

"No promises," Jakon said, and charged.

Clearing the paces between them quickly.

"Figures," Frostine said, "Vile to zee end."

And shattered into icy snow? Snow that smelled of fresh fox?

Jakon growled. "Running away? Figures. Coward to the end."

BOOM!

Right behind him. A furry back smashed into his.

Hard.

Shoving him forward several paces. The smell of vaporized iron?

Jakon turned around. "Saphira?"

Saphira was on her knees. Gasping.

"Frostine," Saphira said, "can. telejump. More than lightning. Hurry. My sisters. They—"

Puff!

Back into his deck.

And only few paces away Frostine looked as shocked as he was himself.

No. No more hesitating.

He charged. Quick. Careful.

A swing. Up at her head.

Frostine vanished again.

But Jakon continued his swing. Swinging up above his head.

CRACKLE!

Lightning crackled into his sword. Absorbed by it.

Powering him up better than any bout of R&R. His body burned with energy. Energy he'd need to save. Save for taking down more than just this vixen witch.

For taking down that dragon too.

A dragon that roared again.

But only watched?

"FROSTINE!" the dragon said, "DO NOT FAIL ME AGAIN!"

"Again?" Frostine said, and the fear in her face as she looked at her Dragon Lord, so genuine Jakon almost felt sorry for her.

Almost.

(No wonder Azura preferred being a carded monster girl.)

(Scarlet too.)

But Jakon didn't hesitate. In that instant of distraction he struck. Slashing through her chest armor.

Frostine yelped. Stumbled back.

She struck back with lightning. Lightning that went wild. Got absorbed by his sword. Boosted his power for the next strike.

Through her chest.

She coughed up blood. "To fail twice ..."

"I should let you die," Jakon said, "But a promise is a promise, even by a half dwarf."

He slipped out an empty card. It transformed into a dagger and he stabbed her with it.

Frostine tried to speak, but only coughed up more blood. Didn't get carded either.

Yet.

So Jakon twisted both blades. Loud wet cracks came from her chest. Forcing more blood up out of her mouth.

Then Frostine exploded into ice and lightning?

"What the ..." Jakon said.

A sinister giggle came from behind him.

"To zeenk," Frostine said, "you almost had me."

Jakon turned. But too late.

Freezing blades sliced around his back. His side as he turned. Faced Frostine. Stumbling backwards.

His back roasting with electric. Shocking him full of lightning. Jolted him. Shuttering. Uncontrollably.

He fell on his ass. Crawled backwards.

His blade lost. A few paces away. Too far to reach.

And Frostine loomed over him. Her claw extenders bloody. With his blood.

"Now your turn," Frostine said, "to die—"

An arrow sprouted from her eye. Red feathered with a green shaft?

Frostine yowled. Just as another arrow sprouted form her other eye.

She snarled. "Not like thees!"

But Jakon already had another empty card out. Transformed it to a dagger.

A dagger he plunged into her chest.

Twisted hard and sharp.

That loud wet crack. She coughed up blood.

"No ... I ..." Frostine said.

"Lost," Jakon said, "Accept your fate and—"

"Vee die together!" Frostine said and crackle?

Her claw extenders. Overcharged with blue lightning!

And Jakon was too close to retreat.

Frostine slashed at him.

When another arrow sprouted down through her throat. Forced her to gurgle. Stumble back.

And the most gorgeous girl Jakon ever saw jumped down at the vixen witch. Despite that suggestively stretchy minidress with minimum coverage, so minimum her waist-long sky-blue hair covered more, yet the gorgeous girl managed to gracefully land both her low-heeled boots right on the ends of both those red-feathered arrows. Shoving them both deep into the vixen's eyes.

CRUNCH!

The arrows got shoved deep into the vixen's head. Right into her brain.

PUFF!

Frostine was carded.

But also tripped up the gorgeous blue-haired girl.

Till Jakon lunged. Caught her.

And wow, was she so soft and warm, yet ... delicate. She even gasped. Blushed at his arms. Her eyes were as wide as the sky and just as sky blue. Just like her hair. Sky blue. Her warm breath even smelled a good bit rosy.

Like a rosy mead? Was she drunk?

She even smiled nervously at him.

"Thanks ..." she said, meekly.

"I should be thanking you," Jakon said, "For feathering that vixen at the perfect moment."

"Not perfect," the gorgeous girl said, "Or you wouldn't of been hurt. Here ... I have something. For your ... bleeding."

From between her big breasts, from out of a pink, very cheek-warmingly visible bra she slipped out a glass vial of red liquid something. She popped the cap off, and poured it quickly into his mouth and ... WOW.

So rosy good and—ack! Throating burningly bad.

And very, *very* alcoholic.

But Jakon refused to cough. A dwarf had to stay strong.

Instead, he smiled back at the gorgeous girl.

"Wonderful," he said, "My back ... feels better too."

And it did. Like the wounds were knitting together by themselves. A touch itchy, but nothing compared to the pain early. This potion was even better the potions of the hedge-witch healer Jakon and his mom's students often went to after serious enough injuries. Only serious injuries because her healing was too expensive for the more minor injuries, but she did heal their scars, whether they wanted them healed or not.

The gorgeous girl smiled again. Even more.

"I ..." she said, and gulped.

Her breathe. It must be making him drunk too.

No. Drunker. That potion did a real clobbering on him.

But Jakon still stroked her soft cheek. Guided her strawberry lips toward his. She didn't resist at all. No. She let him guide her to him.

Let him kiss her. Wet and warm.

Her gasp. "I ..."

"A reward," Jakon said, "for saving me twice."

The girl gulped. "I'm ... Sky. You're?"

"Jakon. At your service."

Sky took a deep breathe. "I ... I came here to ... to train in ... in."

But kissed him back. Just as warm and wet.

"A little love," she said, "after battle, won't hurt, right?"

"Right," Jakon said, "might even help."

They both laughed. Undressing each other. Awkwardly nervous but ... they embraced. Giggled at each other. In a playful way. Too embarrassed for words. For now.

Naked and yet, the girl pressed herself against him. So warm and soft. She panted quiet and so, so cutely. Her breasts against his chest so heart-thumpingly great. Her touch everywhere was so soft and gentle. He never imagined it would be like this. Like a glove of sensual bliss was over him, especially down there. He even grabbed her behind. And helped. With the pumping. The quiet pants. And the joy.

Even to the sweaty climax.

She sighed. Pressing her ample chest against his strong one even snugger. Her cheeks were very, very red. Embarrassed red.

"Oh no," she said, "I'm still drunk. From the rose mead. And the battle ... I never ... fought a real battle. And ..."

Jakon kissed her again. "No worries. A dwarf never kisses and tells."

She giggled. Kissed him back as wet and warm as he ever

longed for in a kiss. Dreamed of. Better than any kiss in a dime dreadful even.

"And an elf," she said, "never lets a first love escape unscathed."

Elf ... his heart stopped.

Her ears even ... oh no, like super-soft thin daggers, from straight out of the sides of her head ... she.

She was an elf girl?!

CHAPTER 24
DRAKOTH

Drakoth curled tight around the top spire of the Dirlop Mountain. As if he was squeezing the life out of a giant mouse, but the spire was too much like a granite spike into the sky, even if it was on the cooler side. For now. His flame wasn't needed.

Yet.

Along the steep craggy slopes the wind carried the smell of dead warthoggish orc and dying dwarf. Flesh he would normally roast and eat, but no. Not this time.

Not when his victory was so close.

Soon he'd celebrate by munching that tasty looking elf girl that was mating with that dwarf boy.

But not yet.

The carding of Frostine and so quickly only delayed the true assault to sunset. When the true troopers would assault the dwarves. Conquer their mountain.

Pearl and her corpse would aid them. Along with the dead fox men. The dead orc bodies.

The seeds within them had already rooted. Seeding deep into the stone of the mountain.

While the smell, the cries of agony, it was more than enough for Drakoth to savor his victory, even if it seemed, for the moment, that his forces had lost.

No.

Their goal was only to destroy the barrier to the next invasion force, but without giving away that they were not alone.

Their second goal was to provide corpses to seed the first stage of the next attack. Corpses that could not be burned nor moved. All because the seeds of the blood rose within them have now rooted deep within their dead bodies.

Not even those vixens knew how expandable they were. They were just fertilizer for the blood rose. A rose that would sprout another castle from this very mountain.

Conquer it like none had before.

Those snake-bone armors gave those snow vixens far too much confidence, but he had plenty of such vixens, and other creatures, to replace them.

They fought well enough, if a bit disappointing.

Their destruction of the walls. The barriers. That was enough.

Even if Frostine was carded. Her seed not rooted. Yet.

The orc invasion was only to soften the dwarves. Seeding what was coming—the blood rose and its castle. Make the dwarves think those pathetically undead orcs were the key invasion.

Not the coming forces.

The rosy fragrance was a warning, but only those with the most potential could even smell it. Potential to destroy his new creation: Blood Rose Castle. So Drakoth would hunt them down personally, when the time came, but for now, his assassins would soon arrive.

Blend into the weakened defenses.

Gather the info Drakoth needed. Before slaying the few captives that needed slaying.

Like Frostine and her scarlet vixens. After removing them from their cards.

Those wretched vixens should of died on the field. Not let themselves be carded, but that snake-bone armor was more than armor.

Soon they learn the price of their so-called failure.

Drakoth chuckled. That so few dwarves were killed by Frostine's orcs ... all because she was so reluctant to kill.

The softhearted bitch. Even after Drakoth paid a handsome sum to those dwarven outlaws to ransack her home. Card a handful of specific beast elves. Let specific beast elves live, while other were slain. Killing those outlaws to gain the survivors' trust ... simple, and pathetic.

Soon it would be Frostine's turn to die. Properly this time.

Along with her scarlet vixens.

The loss of those vixen witches was expected. No, needed. The snow and scarlet vixens had the most potential to seed the best vines of the blood rose. Pearl and the fox men weren't enough. Not even the horde of now dead orcs.

Soon the suicidal beast elves would arrive. Cultists willing to die by their own hands at sunset. All in utter awe of dragons like Drakoth. Pathetic worms. But useful ones.

They'd seed what Frostine and her scarlet vixens were meant to. So just a delay. Nothing more.

But this spire, soon it would be the perfect stem for the greatest castle of all, the Rose Blood Castle.

A castle soon full of horrors, of the darkest elves and of dwarves turned darkest of trolls.

And more.

Soon this Dirlop Mountain would be the latest roost for Blood Rose Castle.

And nothing more.

CHAPTER 25
JAKON

Jakon smelled such a strong rosy fragrance now, like those rose bouquets mom loved on her birthday, but it couldn't be coming from Sky. Sure, she was a gorgeous elf girl so her natural smell would be some kind of plant or fruit, but there wasn't a touch of alcohol to the aroma, and wow, did that girl smell of alcohol right now.

Not that he minded but just her fumes were enough to get him drunk, no, *drunker* than whatever that healing potion she fed him did. He could still taste its rosy goodness and alcoholic searing wow. He'd have to give elves some respect for brewing that kind of drink. Even dad ... really might. As reluctant as he would be. Especially if he didn't get a taste of it himself.

By now Jakon and Sky were both dressed again. Mostly. Sky kept her bra and hat in her pouch now. A pouch shaped like a pink cutesy fat heart. Stuffed full with his jerkin too.

Since Sky seemed to love his bare hairy chest as much as he loved her ample soft breasts.

Especially how her minidress covered so little of them.

But still, half naked or not, they both were ready for battle. Together. Mostly.

If it came to that.

Standing beside each other, they both stayed hidden behind a large craggy boulder to avoid the gaze of that scarlet dragon who was still curled around the top spire of Dirlop Mountain.

One of his arms stayed wrapped securely around Sky's slim soft waist. Just like a hero from his dime dreadfuls. Getting the gorgeous girl and quickly too. Just like she kept an arm around his. With drunk smile and a dagger in her other hand. While he carried his magical short sword again.

And their best hope to survive if that dragon started hunting them. Decided to avenge its student's defeat.

Dragon flame was magical enough that, hopefully, his magical sword could absorb it too.

If not ... they'd think of something.

As heart racing chilly as that was. Helped by how her sharp but soft and gentle dagger ear poked the side of his head good and prickly. Reminding him again and again that an actual blade would be far worse.

Good thing Jakon knew this crop of boulders from childhood. For years, as a little kid, he'd play adventurer and fight imaginary monsters, and sometimes, even fight his own carded monsters. Or even better, Gunter would arrange the adventure beforehand using his monster cards as real-life enemies. Just like what Jakon would do for Gunter.

And to make a dramatic ambush perfect, a dwarf needed to know the layout of the land perfectly. Understand where and when others would try going. How they'd go. How fast. When they'd be careful.

And when they'd be careless.

There were plenty of times when Gunter or Jakon would climb up to the top spire and plant some monster card there, (to the chagrin of the wall guards) like some fantastic dragon or something else large and scary, until they finally went too far (a Three-headed Violet Titan Dragon that was so big it nearly broke the spire) and got them a serious walloping by the mayor himself.

But thanks to those crazy shenanigans so long ago, Jakon actually knew the way up the mountain without getting spotted by the real and true dragon now coiled around the top spire.

Thankfully, after a quick hush for warning, Sky accepted his lead without question.

Probably too drunk to question him, but trust was trust, and a dwarf didn't question his luck—unless it was an obvious trap.

And the twitching orc corpses ... something was off about them. They twitched and shifted too much. Their chests were expanding too much.

More and more. Far quicker than from any kind of bloating from rot. Some didn't seem entirely dead yet either.

Their moans and groans too awfully lively. Their eyes moving.

It was like something ... tentacled was struggling to rip out of them?

But what?

Even Sky squirmed at the sight. Shuttered in what seemed disgusted sadness. And everyone knew how much elves and orcs hated each other. Savored the suffering of the other. Least according to the dime dreadfuls, and they had been right about orcs and beast elves. So far.

So Jakon made a point to navigate far away from the strangely bloating orc corpses. As far as he could manage.

Without putting them within sight of the scarlet dragon.

Except the sudden wet booms ...

Thick green vines erupted from the orc corpses in sight. Vine with razor sharp looking thorns. Leaves fringed with blood red. Even buds. All growing larger and larger.

The rosy fragrance grew even stronger now. Even more than the awful smell of dead orc.

Jakon forced himself to gulp. Finally speak up.

"That rosy fragrance," he said, "that's not you, is it?"

Sky gasped. "No ... I thought ... y-you mean, that's not normal around here?"

"No," Jakon said, "It must be those vines. Some kind of rose vine. You happen to read anything about the Blood Rose Castle of Doom?"

"Ooo," Sky said, "I did. On the way here, but ..."

"You have a copy on you?" Jakon said.

"No ... it got ruined on the way here," Sky said, "Sorry."

"No need to apologize," Jakon said, "We'll head to my room and grab my copy."

"Ooo good," Sky said, "How much further?"

"Not much," Jakon said, "just a little further. There's just a little problem, but ..."

"Little or big," Sky said, "we'll find a way around it."

She giggled a touch, and gave him another strawberry sweet kiss.

CHAPTER 26
JAKON

That kiss from Sky gave Jakon the boost in courage he needed more than he realized. His heart was racing already, but now in a good way again. His legs were now as solid as the ground beneath him again. And the boulders looming around them shielded them from any embarrassing onlookers, giving them the privacy a pair of lovers loved to have when together.

He'd even slay that scarlet dragon to protect Sky.

If it came to that.

If.

The moans, groans, and booms of orcs bursting into thick rose vines, no, Jakon needed to focus on the new danger now. These vines were forming a tentacled hedge maze along the whole slope of Dirlop Mountain.

No telling what the dragon's plot was—unless he

grabbed that dime dreadful book and quickly. Figure out what this scheme was.

Before it was too late.

Sky probably had a hunch but clearly she wanted to double check something before saying anything and sending them off in the wrong direction.

So Jakon led Sky around the last of the boulders and ... oh crap. The outside wall to his room had been destroyed in the earlier attack. From the bolt of lightning. Enough that instead of a wall, there was a huge jagged opening. Like a rounded indent of a cliff. Difficult to climb—and the risk of being seen by the scarlet dragon ... not good.

Not good at all.

The closest ledge, the floor to his actual room in fact, was a few paces beyond his reach, even if he jumped as high as he could manage.

And not many boulders intact enough to shield them from prying eyes.

Behind them, from out of the endless boulders, more vines were rising up to the sky. Thick and thorny. Buds here and there. Buds bigger than any dwarf's head and still growing bigger. And bigger. More red. Blood red.

The rosy aroma was even stronger now. Enough that it smothered the alcoholic fumes on Sky's own rosy breath. Even when she was hugging his side cozy and warm for support. Her dagger-ears softly poking the side of his head gently but prickly scratchy and so, so cute.

But wow, did he love her ... suggestive minidress right

now and all the peachy beautiful soft skin it showed. Including plenty of breast and thigh and sexy side tummy and sigh.

Focus.

On surviving. Then they could have more sex. Survive and more sex, definitely.

Good reason to survive unscathed. So he could be scathed plenty by his first elven love. The best kind of scathing. Probably. Hopefully.

"Ooo" Sky said, "You r-r-room. It's up there? I can jump it. And help you up. Okay?"

Jakon nodded. "Be careful. The dragon ..."

"I know," Sky said, "Dragons love to eat elf girls like me. One ate my cousin, and she ... was as pretty as me, until and ... another got my niece. I ..."

Jakon kissed her lips. "I'll protect you. With this."

And he held up his magical short sword. They both looked at it and she giggled with some obvious relief.

"And when you do," Sky said, "I'll fuck you some more—later."

And she gave him another wet kiss on his lips.

"But first ... a nice look up there," she said, and let go.

Leapt high up. Giving him a very clear view of her pink panties from below. Her giggly glance downward, a wiggle of her fine, fine rear and rubbing of her sexy bare thighs, and to top it off, a very giggly approval of his face warming redder than the most scarlet scales of that dragon.

So with a jump and helpful heave, Jakon was up in his room again.

But the slopes of Dirlop Mountain ...
A thicket of thick thorny rose vines.
And getting thicker. With no end in sight.

CHAPTER 27
IVY

Ivy was shocked, *shocked* at just how **many** gemstones shined throughout the whole entire ceiling. Really. So much light, and soooo many colors, all from so many precious stones. No wonder those dragons wanted to conquer this place. They loved shiny gemstones almost as much as they loved munching cute girls like Ivy.

Kinda like what happened to her peace-loving oldest sis.

No point in loving peace if that meant a dragon could eat you any moment it felt like it, and dragons loved themselves a tasty looking girl, but not guys as much, for some weird reason.

(Maybe they were just perverts at heart.)

That the spikes in the ceiling dripped so much water everywhere, she was already very drippy wet from her swim that turned out, not to be so secret as she hoped.

Far less secret.

The smell of blood and worse chilled her more than excited right now. Not very warrior-like but with her own kind used as monster cards, and her being the only survivor, unless Helga did some veeeery fancy talking, Ivy was in **very** deep trouble.

Maybe Ivy could just surrender, technically, and convince Helga to give Ivy to Jakon as some kind of war loot and then ... well ... trust Jakon to the do the right thing and ... well ... not release her, of course. Even a dwarf wouldn't go that far, but treat her better than, well, alchemy material to be, or some sex slave or whatnot.

Yet Ivy couldn't keep her tail from slinking too low. Too much like when she faced the elders again and again and again and knew she had no chance of coming out ahead.

At all.

The gray cloud was settling down and clearing up and woh, more dead dwarves than ... and tigermite warriors that .... those injuries ... Helga did them in and Ivy couldn't blame her for it.

Ivy was lucky Helga didn't do her in with them.

But that fox guy dead on the ground ... he was bloating up far too fast. Like something tentacled was trying to burst out of him. Ivy was backing away, of course, since curiosity killed the cat, especially if that cat was an overeager tigermite, but Helga, despite staring at the dead bloating fox guy, she wasn't backing up enough. Not much at all.

And there wasn't much of anyone else left here right now. The cries of alarm and more echoed from a distance away, of course, since this cavern looked crazy big and wide. And as the cloud settled away, lots of shops too. The dwarves here, dead, dying, or running ... not warriors but shoppers. Going about their daily business. Not at all ready for the ambush this fox guy pulled on them.

Unlike tigermites. Who were always ready for an ambush.

Even by allies. Friends.

By anyone—ack!

The fox guy exploded. Releasing thick green tentacles—no. *Vines*. Thorn vines thick and curling and vicious.

But also ... the dead tigermites exploded?!

Each and every one. All into thick thorn vines. Vines that expanded without end.

"Helga!" Ivy said, "Behind you!"

Ivy moved pouncing fast. Grabbing Helga.

Saving her from those charging vines.

"Ivy ..." Helga said but didn't struggle in her grip.

"I'll surrender later," Ivy said, "We need to get out of here! Like now. Those vines. I don't think they'll stop. They looked familiar but ..."

"Familiar?" Helga said, and sighed. "I think ... from a castle?"

Ivy gasped, her ears perking up so high they hurt.

"Heeeey yeah!" Ivy said, "A castle. From this morning. On Razorspine Peak."

Helga gasped this time. "Then Jakon ... oh no. Ivy I need you to find Jakon. Protect him. If this is what I think it is, he'll be targeted by what's coming ... I need to warn the mayor and general. Please, I—"

"As you wish!" Ivy said, "I am your student, and now, well, loot something so ..."

"I ..." Helga said, "Don't be silly. You're not loot."

"But tell that to the dwarves ..." Ivy said, "I—what if I wear the collar that prevents me from leaving? Or harming any dwarf? That should keep any dwarf I run into from you know."

Helga sighed. "Those are difficult to remove and—"

"Enough that the dwarves will help me," Ivy said, "not attack me."

Helga sighed, clearly reluctant. "You're right but I might not be allowed to remove it. Not for a long time."

"It's not a slave collar," Ivy said, "Just a ... restraining collar. I'll manage."

Helga kissed her forehead? Yay!

"Thank you," Helga said.

And click. An iron collar was around Ivy's neck. With some very shiny precious glowing amber stones in it.

Ivy let go of Helga. "Where ..."

Helga gave direction and without further delay, Ivy dashed for Jakon's room.

CHAPTER 28
JAKON

Jakon gawked at the bottom shelf, the one chiseled like the solid gray gears he used to love forging before his human side ended that part of his life forever. But now, no, he almost snarled more vicious than any raging beast elf.

Almost.

But silent rage was better sometimes.

Sometimes.

For the cracks and booms of the vines conquering the slopes of Dirlop Mountain ... the dust clouding everything, even making his room a foggy gray ... but it wasn't enough to stop his dwarven vision.

From spotting the horror of his bottom shelf ... all the books were shredded like cheap flimsy paper coleslaw.

Brown rotten coleslaw.

Even the leatherbacks on the shelves above it. None of them were in better shape. No matter the topic, minerals or histories or even bestiaries, they all were all sliced and diced, but nowhere as badly as the dime dreadful paperbacks.

Just bad enough to never be used again.

All those memories of late-night fun … destroyed. Forever.

His whole collection of books … gone. All because that snow vixen Frostine unleashed so many vicious orcs. Orcs with no respect for life or learning.

Jakon almost pounded some of the remaining wall. Almost. But Sky caught his fist. Eased his hand back to his side. Her strength, not bad, not bad at all. Had she been a dwarf woman, she could of trained for smithing herself.

"Jakon," Sky said, and with a sympathetic smirk too, "Don't forget you carded the vixen responsible. A snow vixen of high value … in m-many ways."

Jakon gasped. "You're right. I could summon her now and …"

"Can you compel her to answer?" Sky said, "Truthfully and honestly?"

"No …" Jakon said, "But I know someone who can. Someone who …"

This time, Jakon smirked as well. No need to be the one to punish Frostine. He was an amateur at that too. Let an experienced Interrogator do the deed.

"Let's hurry," he said, and hand-in-hand, he led the way into Dirlop Mountain—or was about it.

When Ivy dashed into his room.

Her strong orange and cream scent stunned him as much as her sudden appearance. Despite her being dripping wet she had that strong lovely smell. She even looked absolutely gorgeous in her cowled bra top and miniskirt ... wait. A miniskirt?! Since when ... she always had form-fitting slacks on before.

And her skin now was so clear and bright now, especially its orange tiger coloring, especially in the light that ...

Ivy gasped. "Outside!"

Jakon turned and ... a hollow blood red sun high in the sky?!

Even the rest of the sky was dark and red and threatening.

Sky gasped loud and clear.

"The Blood Sun Eclipse ..." Sky said, "w-we don't have much time left."

Ivy hopped over. Sniffed Sky? A very loud and very long sniff. Her green eyes going so wide and shocked Jakon ...

"Really?" Ivy said, and glared at Jakon?

Ivy puffed. "I heard elf girls are easy but that's just ridiculous."

That shocked Sky as much as it did Jakon.

"I ..." Sky said, "Better enjoy love. When we can. Never know when we'll die. Right, Jakon?"

"Yeah," Jakon said, and gave Sky's hand a comforting squeeze, "Ivy, that's ..."

"If you want some quick sex," Ivy said, "I don't like, mind, but don't think I'll give up on you so quickly."

Sky giggled. "Ooo, a ... threesome then?"

Then shocked Jakon and Ivy.

"Um ... maybe?" Ivy said, and cocked her hips in that miniskirt that woh, did ivy have some niiiiice legs. Her form-fitting slacks really left more to the imagination than he realized.

Jakon managed to gulp. "Great. Love the miniskirt, but first let's save Dirlop Mountain."

That perked Ivy's kitty ears high up and gave her a wicked smirk.

"Don't think I'll be as easy to conquer than that elf girl," Ivy said.

"Conquer?" Jakon said, "We're—"

"Not friends anymore," Ivy said, and tapped ... an iron collar around her neck. With amber gemstones that glowed and ...

"A captive collar?" Jakon said, "No, I'll go find a way to get it removed. You should be released and—"

"Your mom," Ivy said, "collared me for my own safety. I'll count as your loot girl, but don't think you'll get a lot of easy sex from me—not without some real you know."

Ivy even purred so suggestively that ... Sky giggled even more suggestively?

Sky squeezed Jakon's waist. "I'll help you too you know, he-he. I've always wanted the right kind of threesome so ..."

Yet Ivy sighed. "Geez, we're soooo supposed to be rivals yet ... *fine.*"

Sky even hopped over to Ivy and gave her a friendly big hug? A hug ivy reluctantly returned.

"I've always w-wanted to a tigermite friend," Sky said, "and lover."

Ivy sighed. "Your drunk. Reeeeeally drunk."

"Still?" Sky said, "I only drank—never mind. Maybe I am. Let's have fun then! (While we can ...)"

Jakon couldn't help but chuckle at Ivy and Sky.

"Let's first save Dirlop Mountain," he said, "Then we can celebrate with all the fun the three of us can have."

CHAPTER 29
JAKON

But fun was soon far from Jakon's mind as they dashed through the narrow winding hallways of Dirlop Mountain. Thankfully so many forked here and there, but they found dead orcs everywhere. All bursting into more and more thick thorny vines that clogged the hallways. Each time the rosy aroma was so strong that Jakon soon made a point to avoid any hallways with that smell coming from it.

That the hallways were dimmer than usual. From gemstones stolen by orc thieves. Clearly pried out. The damage to the surrounding rock clear.

Only dwarves could truly appreciate the genuine value of gemstones, and not just for some pathetic coin.

That the orcs had died for their invasion and thief was only a cold comfort. Especially with the vines bursting them from now. Vines ripping and cracking more and more rock. Sucking in more and more gemstones.

Sending more and more of Dirlop Mountain into darkness.

A darkness that would take years to repair and fix. Years Jakon couldn't do much to help, given his human side and its limitations.

All he could do now was help stop the invasion. Reduce the damage it was doing to the mountain he called home.

Sky and Ivy stayed close behind him. Not saying a word. But clearly ready to support him. Not even questioning the way he seemed to scattered here and there. Finding more and more passages blocked by thorny thick vines.

Their progress was slow.

Too slow.

But it was progress.

When Azura puffed out of her card. The furball looked so much like Frostine, except with sky-blue hair, that Jakon flinched, crouching as if about to be attacked, but no.

Her sadness was too clear.

Even with her blue claw extenders, pouch, and belt, she was bare in the beautiful white fur. Very smutty elf girl style. She didn't even have that snake-bone armor.

Her foxy ears sank even more at his reaction.

"Jakon ..." Azura said.

Jakon nodded. "Sorry, your sisters, they were Frostine and Pearl, right?"

Azura nodded back, but only whimpered. her hands by her ample chest.

Jakon heart sank. "I had to stop Frostine. She—"

"I understand," Azura said, "She ... please let me help question her, and ... maybe ..."

"Spare her the worst?" Jakon said.

Azura nodded. "She's my sister and ... and ..."

"You would of been with them," Jakon said, "On their side had your life gone ... differently. I know. As angry, as furious as I am with Frostine, I won't take her from you. Help me get everything out of Frostine, so we can save Dirlop Mountain, and I'll do my best to unit your cards into one, so you both share the same card."

That really perked Azura up. "Really? Yay! I'll *so* help out."

"We just have to get there," Jakon said, "And soon. If it weren't for all these vines ..."

"Leave that to me!" Azura said, "Hug me everyone. Like I'm your best precious furry doll."

Okay. Jakon did, without hesitating too much, and wow, was she so furry soft and warm and even that gentle scent of fox ... it was ... nice. Nicer than it should of been. Especially after his fight with Frostine and the other beast elves. Sky and Ivy even hugged Azura's sides.

"Ready?" Azura said.

Everyone nodded and—flash!

CHAPTER 30
JAKON

Flash?

A blinding sky-blue flash. Cold as the many mountain blizzards during last winter yet also … refreshing? Like a crisp cold drink on a hot day. But even now, the crisp cold of the flash was being nibbled away from the usual sweltering heat of Dirlop Mountain.

Cracks and scratches rang out, echoing sharply throughout what sounded like narrow tunnels clogged with more and more vines.

And then echoed into a wide cavern? With that familiar drip drip drip in small walled craters …

Ah!

Jakon let go of Azura. No dwarves nearby, yet, but the colorful craters were still naturally barricaded off. They even blocked most of the cavern from their vantage point.

But not the vines already expanding around some of the further craters.

Vines that moved ... funny? Like something, no, *things* invisible smacked them for a brief moment.

As if coming toward them.

"You know where to go?" Jakon said.

Azura nodded, ears sunk, but licked his lips? Sigh. So he handed Azura Frostine's card.

She vanished again. With another flash.

Ivy sighed, folding her arms over her ample chest with another big pout.

"We should of gone with her," Ivy said.

But Jakon drew his magical short sword.

"Enemies incoming," he said, and motioned behind Ivy.

Ivy gasped and turned.

Just in time. Deflected a strike. That spark?

From a dagger?

Clang!

Clang!

Double dagger strikes. From someone slim. Wrapped entirely in dark red.

Ivy deflected them all. With her katars.

While Jakon struck back. Slashing the chest. The enemy dodging.

But not by enough.

Yet the enemy only gasped—until Ivy diced them up. With her katars.

A cry behind Jakon?

Sky saved him. Her scimitars were already in a bow form.

She fired another a bolt. Hit another enemy trying to back-stab Jakon.

Another death cry.

Another enemy down.

Jakon cried out, "Back-to-back!"

All three did so. Facing the new threat. Cutting down red-wrapped enemy after enemy.

Till none remained.

When they all got back. Together. And hissed. All together.

Sky cried out, "No! They're blood elves!"

"Blood elves?" Ivy said.

Jakon gasped. "Vampires! Aim for their hearts!"

The fight began anew. Fierce and bloody. With more than just their weapons hissing now.

A fight Jakon and his companions were losing.

Badly.

Until a blue bolt of lightning shot through all the blood elves. Through their chests. Freezing them into blocks of ice.

And shattering. All into a misty crisp nothing.

With an awfully familiar laugh cackling out in front of Jakon.

And a pair of snow vixen witches back for some action: Azura and Frostine. Together side-by-side. Mere paces ahead of him.

"Zhees blood elves are quite tricky, no?" Frostine said.

Jakon growled, but nodded. A dwarf didn't begrudge some help, no matter the source, especially life-saving help.

Azura perked up. "But we can scent them, right sis?"

"Right," Frostine said, "and just so you know, I do not know anytheeng about these vines. Drakoth told me nothing about them. Or of any attack beyond my own and Pearl's."

Jakon tsked, crouching, listening for more enemies coming, but ...

Azura pouted?

"I can scent she's telling us the truth," Azura said "And she just saved you! You should just accept her. You won that fight. Don't be a spoiled winner."

Azura was ... sigh. Gunter would chuckle at this too. Proud his gift was so important to saving Dirlop Mountain and Jakon.

So he nodded. "You're right. As a reward, I'll see about uniting you two into the same card."

That perked both snow vixens up happy.

And they both licked a kiss on each of his cheeks. So gross ... yet so cute, and nice, actually.

Enough that his cheeks heated away the cool after nip of moisture quickly.

And quickly realized their other problem.

One not so easy to solve—what to do next.

CHAPTER 31
ROSE

Queen Briar Rosendoom chuckled as she strutted up the thick solid rose vine as quietly as a fox prowling up to a tasty overconfident rooster.

The familiar of smell of blood rose, of both blood and rose together, and more crimson the rose, the more death it absorbed, the more blood it would provide her kind, the blood elves, also known as vampires to lesser beings.

The foolish dragon curled on top of this mountain thought it was still in charge. Ha!

But no need to remove that delusion. Yet.

Its blood would soon be ripe enough to harvest. Just like the dwarves here. And even that delicious looking elf girl.

And tigermite girl. Still a virgin. So extra tasty.

Their blood should be enough to extend her own youthful body for another century. The blood of the dwarves should be enough for her servants to extend their youth for another century as well, but dwarves, even their women, were never as delicious as elves and tigermites.

The blood roses were already beginning to bud. Grow big and fat with death. Even if it was only the death of the orcs and a few of those pathetic beast elves.

So far.

And a few dwarves and tigermite men. Not enough ... yet.

But soon more would die. More would feed the blood roses. Let her castle come and establish itself on this peak. Absorb the dragon and stabilize its own existence for another century. That other peak nearby was too barren to support her caste, but this mountain, plenty of life to feast on.

And one measly dragon for another century of a castle none of the lesser races could ever hope to build, let alone maintain.

Such a small price to pay ... Queen Briar almost laughed.

Almost plucked a tasty petal off a lone bud, but no, she continued to kept strutting up to the top. Her leotard of crimson silk was spelled to protect her heart several times over. Besides the scarlet dragon scale plating over her chest. Her blood red hair flow down and whipped about in the wicked wind. Hair she could control herself. Use like savage razor whips, if need be, but she preferred her pair of blood scimitars that could be snapped together by the handle to launch magical bolts of blood and death.

Death that dragon would soon suffer firsthand.

Her crown of golden thorns was protection enough, especially with the spells woven into it to protect her from attacks both physical and nonphysical, magical or mundane.

But she couldn't feed while wearing it. Not yet.

For that she'd need some more alchemy. Most of the gemstones in this very mountain too. And two more snow vixen witches carded for material.

Not a problem. Her spies revealed one snow vixen was already card within this mountain. The other snow vixen, one of the two this pathetic dragon had prepared, but unlike the dead one, one also got carded, saving the queen some effort. Her assassins should retrieve those cards soon enough.

She also permitted her assassins to feed on any dwarf that dared stand in their way.

But not the elf girl, or the tigermite girl. They were hers and hers alone to feast on, and on no else's.

Capturing them, only that was acceptable—as long as they weren't damaged.

Too much.

Death would come quickly to any of her kind that dared defy her. Her crown would ensure that much.

And once she reached the top of this vine, her castle would absorb that foolish dragon. Then the Blood Rose Castle would appear once again.

And their next victory would be assured.

The pathetic dragon looked her way. Dared snort in her direction.

"Blood elf," the dragon dared to said with scorn.

"Bow," the queen said, "or die."

Before the dragon could even sneeze some flame, the queen fired blood bolts into its pathetic eyes.

The lizard was so slow even its roar was interrupted by more of her blood bolts. Right into its gaping maw.

Choking its roar to a pathetic gurgle.

The dragon rasped. "You ... how dare you! I am a Dragon Lord and you are—"

"A Queen of Darkness," Queen Briar said, "and you are just one of many wyrms who think too highly of yourself. Too brainwashed to realize the truth—until we let you."

"Truth?" the dragon said, "There is no truth! Only power. My power! Power that—ack!"

Her bolts all exploded. Their blood cursed. Melting away flesh and bone. Spells weaving themselves for the summoning.

A summoning she finished as easily as killing that pathetic lizard.

And soon the dwarves would follow.

CHAPTER 32
JAKON

Jakon could only make out the closest of the vines grinding heavy against stone wall, but the thick sound and smell, this place would be overrun soon.

And no sign of the dwarves that should normally be here either. Today it should of been busy. The battle against Frostine couldn't of taken him that long. Long enough for everyone to clear, and fight the invading orcs, but the presence of the vines confirmed the orcs had reached this deep.

That rosy fragrance too.

So the dwarves would of retreated deeper into the mountain. Barricaded those less able to fight in the deepest parts. Guarded by the women who were most able to fight. The last defense.

They didn't have much time. Time to take the fight to the enemy. Somehow. Which meant ...

"Frostine," Jakon said, "That dragon, if we take him down—"

"Big if," Frostine said, "but I do not know if that vill be enough. Zee blood elves were not part of zee forces I know anyzeeng about."

Sky cleared her throat. While she kept back against his.

"From what I r-read ..." Sky said, "but I don't know if it's t-true, that the blood elves want blood, our blood to stay young and powerful. Th-they'll need the dragon's blood to feed their castle. To keep it in one solid place for a while."

"Ah, zhat does sound familiar," Frostine said, "Rumor here and there did reach me. Beast elves that failed my previous Masters tended to be fed not just to dragons, but to blood elves, especially to blood elves. Very unpleasant death."

Azura perked up?

"I know," Azura said, "Let's telejump to that secluded spot Ivy loved to hide in."

Jakon nodded, sheathing his sword for now.

"Good idea," Jakon said, "That's close to the peak that dragon was curled around, but hidden from sight."

Ivy huffed, glaring at Jakon.

"You told these furballs about that?" Ivy said, "Really?"

Azura hopped over to Ivy and giggled so wicked silly Jakon didn't have the heart to break the news to Ivy himself and ruin Azura's fun.

"I heard it all," Azura said, "Back as a card. He brought me with him today. He-he. And—ah! Frostine?"

Frostine had grabbed Azura from behind?

"Enough chit chat, little sis," Frostine said, "Vee need to go. Now. Those vines vill crush us all if vee do not hurry."

"Ooo, yeah," Azura said, "Sorry. Let's all telejump together. Group hug one more time!"

Sigh.

But Frostine was right, again, so ...

CHAPTER 33
JAKON

Once the group hug was over once again, Jakon took a tally of their location, since the best offensive required a grasp of their surroundings. And their surroundings ... were, what the ... green walls?!

Like fresh green vines. Lined together. Straight as a hammer handle, thick as his own head, and woven together with smaller leafy tendrils. All forming a wall that loomed so high it ran into pitch utter darkness. The rosy fragrance, it was so strong, from everywhere, it was like a thick miasma. Worse than a heavily perfumed elf girl.

(Not that he minded Sky's lovely natural perfume but ...)

The twisting clear pond was still here. Craggy tall boulders too. But around the edges of the hot steaming water were red tiles similar to layered rose petals.

Blood red rose petals.

All as large as the largest dwarf's feet. If not a bit larger.

Sky screamed?!

A red-haired elf lady hugged Sky from behind. Hissing with vampire fangs out. And a golden crown of thorns was on her head.

"My meal arrived so early," the red-haired elf lady said, "Perfect."

Jakon whipped out his short sword.

Charging.

When Ivy cried out. Her katars flying off her hands.

The red-haired lady already had a spinal tail of blood curled around Ivy's neck. Its razor tip pressed hard against her throat.

"Uh uh uh," the red-hair lady said, "Such rude behavior in front of the Queen. You need to be punished ... kill the furballs. NOW."

But both Azura and Frostine puffed. Reverting to their card form in Jakon's deck.

"Oh," the red-haired queen said, "I almost forgot. Almost. Give me your deck, boy, and I'll make your death ... quick and pleasant."

Jakon growled. "A dwarf never—"

Ivy gagged. The queen's blood tail squeezing her throat hard.

But she still managed to speak.

"Let her ... kill me," Ivy said, "and then ... kill her!"

"Never," Jakon said, "Ivy, I ... I ..."

"Uh uh uh," the red-haired queen said, "naughty kitty. That yummy scent. Half tigermite, half elf girl, and all so tasty

I'd be remiss not to drink you all down. NOW DROP THAT SWORD, BOY."

Ivy gasped, struggled against the queen's blood tail.

"Love me? I know …" Ivy said, "but I … lost to Sky. Plutonic girlfriend nonsense … I should of … fucked you. Like she did. Right away. And …"

The queen sighed, shaking her head.

"Oh? A lover's spat?" the queen said, "How silly. You're enemies. Capture and rape the other. That's how—"

The queen squeezed Sky so hard wet cracks rang out from within her.

Jakon cried out. "Sky!"

The queen simply chuckled sinister. Her hands transform into blood talons. Ripped into Sky's sides. The pure bliss on the queen's face …

"This elf girl dies first," the queen said, "unless you drop that sword. I'll leave enough blood for the girl to survive, a bit longer at least. Too bad only the tigermite girl is a virgin. Virgin blood tastes the *best.*"

Jakon clutched the sword harder, and harder … and gulped. Time for one last gambit.

"Ivy," Jakon said, "as much as it's hard to believe this, you're my naughtiest girl of my dreams, come true."

Ivy pouted. "Really? *Now's* the time you … wait, isn't Sky …"

Sky was in so much pain it was clear she hadn't heard him, thankfully.

But Jakon sighed anyway, nodded, and dropped his blade.

"There," Jakon said, "Now—"

The queen chuckled even more sinister. "Kick it over. NOW."

Jakon did so.

The queen stomped one foot on the sword.

"Good," the queen said, "Now die!"

But PUFF!

Behind the queen. A red cherry-scented cloud. Revealing Scarlet. Her bow drawn and loaded.

Feathering the queen in the back.

The queen screamed.

Giving Jakon an instant to react.

To charge.

Faster than any bladework.

The queen flung Ivy at him.

Hard.

But Jakon caught her. His dwarven might not to be under-estimated.

Just as the queen whipped her spinal tail of blood at Scarlet.

Who dodged it. Quickly. And puffed back into Jakon's deck.

Just as Ivy leapt out of Jakon's grip. Lunging for Sky.

Sky flung her head back. Right into the queen's face. Smashing their heads together.

The queen's cry of agony. The moment Ivy needed to strike the queen. With her claws. Sending a huge splash of blood away.

And her powerful pawed feet flung Jakon's sword back to him.

Just as the queen's tail shot through Ivy's gut. Up into her back. Lifting her up. While Ivy struggled. Gagged out blood.

Twitching and shuttering as if dying.

"AAAAHHHHH," the queen said, as both her claws and tail grow even more crimson.

She was drinking the blood of both girls.

In such bliss.

Distracted bliss. Her injuries healing quickly. Too quickly.

And the moment Jakon needed to catch his blade. Dash over.

And cleave the queen from her crown down to her evil heart.

Leaving her to burn to ash.

CHAPTER 34
JAKON

Distance death cries rang out from everywhere. Worse than the last battle field it was. High pitched elven screams, and they all even wretched Jakon and his iron gut uneasy. Cutting down his appetite for his mom's coming meal of corned beef sandwiches down, some, but only some.

A few bellowed like dying trolls. Short but powerful trolls. The kind no lone dwarf cared to face alone. Tales of valor and legend came from facing them down. Chasing them from the caves of squalor they lodged themselves in. Ambushing travelers and dwarves alike.

All those cries came from behind the green vine walls. Its entire height. From the pitch utter darkness they loomed up into.

All those minions dying with their awful queen.

Even a few came below the rose petal floor. Cries that

died out quicker than those above. Cut off prematurely. As if cut by. Killed as they were dying.

And not all were death cries. A familiar deep horn rumbled loud through the floor. The war horn of Dirlop Mountain.

For the counterattack.

Cries of victorious dwarves pushing onward.

Rumbles erupted above Jakon, up from that looming high darkness. Rumbles that were more fierce than a starving dwarf's stomach, and Jakon was hungry by now. Very hungry.

The rumbles were rough enough to wobble Jakon good, even if he was a solid dwarf, so he could stand it plenty. Just like his dad drilled into him long ago when training as a smith.

The rosy fragrance even started fading too. Like a dying bouquet of roses. Like the roses mom once forget to get rid of far too long. The rosy smell was fading back to a heavy elf girl stink that even Sky could of been proud of, rather than an outright miasma that even made a sturdy dwarf a tad dizzy.

But not dizzy enough to notice how Sky was able to sit up, while Ivy still lay crumbled on the ground where the queen had dropped her.

So Jakon dashed over to Ivy first.

Ivy moaned. Cleary in pain. The smell of roasted flesh ... no. That wound in her gut. In her back. Big but not bloody. No. That ashed death of the queen somehow had also cauterized Ivy's deep wounds.

And more. Some of her insides.

Ivy gasped. "Jakon ... nice take down but ..."

She coughed, gagging, but nothing came up. Not even blood. Just the smell of roasted flesh on her breath.

"Ivy," Jakon said kneeling beside her, "I'll—"

"No," Ivy said, "I'm done for. Card me. So I can fight another day, k?"

Suddenly, several paces away, Sky coughed so loudly, like she was choking, and then gasping for breath.

"Wait," Sky said, "I—"

She coughed again, but crawled over quickly. Really quickly. Even for her wounds that ... wounds that were healed?

Yet her breath was so rosy and yet so alcoholic ... but in her hand ... trembling drunk hand ...

"I," Sky said, "A healing potion. One more left."

Jakon snatched it. "Sky, thanks, you're a life saver. In more ways than one."

Sky giggled. Her cheeks were as rosy red as her breathe was rosy alcoholic.

"I won't," Sky said, "lose to. that big boobed. tigermite girl. threesome. today. later ..."

And Sky passed out?

Jakon caught her. Eased her to the ground, and gave her forehead a gentle kiss.

"Rest," Jakon said, "You've earned it."

"Not a kissy lip kiss?" Sky whispered.

Wow. Okay. So Jakon gave he the wettest warmest kiss he could. Right on her lips. Letting her sigh content and into a deep sleep.

Jakon hurried back over to Ivy.

"It's your lucky day," Jakon said, and just as Ivy gasped, he poured it down her throat.

Ivy jolted. Shuttered. Flinched.

Her injuries ... mending by themselves. Closing in.

Vanishing.

Ivy gasped again. Deep and shocked, yet she grinned so happy, yet also so pouty ... she even sighed.

"Looks like," Ivy said, "I owe Sky that threesome, but ... my first time. The two of us. Alone. Sort of?"

"I ..." Jakon said, but couldn't help but smile a bit perverted.

"Undress me," Ivy said, "Better make sure I'm all healed up. That no other injuries need caring."

"Of course," Jakon said, and helped her to sit up.

How she managed to slip his slacks off at the same time ... not that he resisted. At all.

"Here," Ivy said, "help me remove my cowled bra top. The string in back ..."

"It's all ruined," Jakon said, "That queen ... I'd kill her again, but—"

"In that case," Ivy said, "You might as well do what you've wanted for so long."

"Wow," Jakon said, "really?"

"Really," Ivy said, "Go mighty super dwarf boy and tear my bra top off. Get that pervy dream out of your system, k?"

Jakon didn't hesitate. Using the hole the queen's tail made in the back of her bra top, where it ruined the string that tied the top snuggly on, Jakon grabbed the silky strong fabric and with a mighty heave and bellow, he ripped her top in half.

And completely off.

That Sky giggled and even clutched her own chest ... and sighed so lustfully ...

What an elf girl. Least she wasn't the jealous type.

Or third wheel type.

Ivy whistled, perking her kitty ears high up.

"Impressive," ivy said, "That fabric isn't flimsy either."

"I could tell," Jakon said, "Armor quality. Even if it didn't cover so little of you."

Ivy purred. "Too expensive so ... grab my boobs. And enjoy, you know."

She grabbed his hands and guided them to her obese breasts. So warm and soft and heart-thunking dream come true kind of—Jakon gave them a gentle but firm squeeze.

Ivy let out a blissful pant.

Again.

And again.

And again.

Jakon kissed her slim neck. Down to her slim shoulders.

"Sounds like," Jakon said, "You wanted this as much as I did."

"Yeah, but," Ivy said, "once you have me, will you want me again?"

"I never thought," Jakon said, "you'd be so insecure."

Yet he gave her obese breasts another firm squeeze.

Ivy let out another blissful pant.

And another.

And sighed. Blissfully.

"Well," Ivy said, "Let's find out. My miniskirt. No. No need to let go. I'll slip it off and—ah!"

Ivy giggled as Jakon slipped his hand underneath her miniskirt. From behind. Feeling up her fine, fine ass.

She purred. "Just take them off. I ... okay, I'll-heeeey. Careful with the tail."

Her kitty tail smacked his stomach. Once. Twice.

But he grabbed it. Gently.

Gave its tip a sweet little kiss.

While Ivy slipped out of her miniskirt, and surprise, surprise.

"No panties?" Jakon said, "Who's the naughty one?"

Ivy giggled. "I am. Now sheath your blade in me, the right way."

Clutching her breasts and waist, Jakon guided her onto him. Sheathing again and again. His trouser blade piercing her virgin defenses and erupting with warm wet joy.

They both let out a blissful gasp.

And settled in each other's arms.

CHAPTER 35
JAKON

akon was finally back in his familiar anvil of a kitchen. The walls were still curved just right and the diamonds sheened bright and beautifully as anywhere in Dirlop Mountain should. As beautiful as Sky was now glowing, outside and in, even as she stayed in her lovely minidress, as much as she clearly wanted to slip out of it again.

Just like Ivy now too. Both girls eager to go smutty lover for him now. The promised threesome coming sooner than hoped.

The black iron rose of a table even only had three chairs. But they were all black iron and too dangerous for Sky to go near. Maybe even Ivy. Since they all knew now she was half elf.

Sky claimed she could handle the iron. Elves that left their homeland had to train for iron resistance, so they wouldn't get poisoned by food cooked in iron utensils, or getting brushed by a careless jackass.

Ivy clearly had some resistance, given her katars were steel. But Jakon would ensure they'd soon be good dwarven steel.

Ivy was already fondling the solid heavy table. Clearly admiring the intricate rosy design up close and personal. Her green eyes were so big and curious and loving it all—especially the removal of her collar. His mom put in the right word for her, and on top of her help in dealing with the blood elves … Ivy was essentially pardoned by the mayor and granted permission for a marriage-to-be with Jakon.

Just like Sky. Somehow she got a marriage-to-be and the pardon needed to escape whatever trouble would of come from a double marriage to a single dwarf.

So two fiancées … and very much aligned together now.

Yet Sky still kept her distance from all the black iron. As if reluctant to test her good her iron resistance was, but Jakon couldn't blame her. Just being here took plenty of bravery. And she proved herself a worthy warrior and wife during the battle.

That Azura and Frostine were both conscribed into curing the poisons used by that fox warrior minion. That they both were being worked to trim down the big thick rose vines everywhere.

Good for them.

Now that Frostine was properly carded, the mayor permitted her to live on. As long as she did her part in rebuilding and maintaining Dirlop Mountain.

Even Scarlet got to celebrate with some heavy drinking.

(And some not-so-secret sex afterwards with him. To get it out of her system, supposedly, and Sky simply giggled at them both, and had joined in, which threw Scarlet off more than anyone expected.)

But now it was time for their victory meal.

Corned beef sandwiches. Warm, greasy and delicious.

The best kind of sandwiches.

For the best kind of girls a guy could have.

About the Author

Widely traveled, Jonathan Evan Hudson spends as much time studying life as he does writing gripping tales of fantastic adventures. From the giant redwoods of California to the deserts of Israel, his thrilling stories all draw on first-hand experiences and expand them with the fantastic and his acclaimed creativity.

Be the first to know!
For the updates and more:
www.JonathanEvanHudson.com

youtube.com/@jonathanevanhudson
tiktok.com/@jonathan.evan.hudson

A War Of Lust And Oak

Read Now!

Martial Art Of The Phantom Saber

Read Now!

Succubus Slash

Read Now!

The acclaimed Jonathan Evan Hudson weaves an unforgettable tale of thrilling action and adventure spiced with fast-burning romance and doused deep in epic fantasy.

Enter Miles Mayhem. Rich in friends and enemies. And a fat boy badass in the sword.

A seriously delicious smell of bacon and eggs smothered in spiced razor-hot cheddar signals celebration—and serious trouble ahead.

Trouble beyond anything Miles ever expected.

The perfect epic fantasy novel. A genre-enlarging feast for fans of sexy action and fabulous adventure. Read *Succubus Slash* now!

Sword Master Of Honey Heart Resort

Read Now!

Into Shadow Forest

Read Now!

A diamond in the rough the bestselling Jonathan Evan Hudson weaves a thrilling tale from explosive beginning to satisfying end in the awe-inspiring land of Grandcrest.

The talented twenty-something sword master Romeo Bladell yearns for love and adventure.

And at the musty edges of Shadow Forest. Near the towering high oaks bearded like stout old dwarves. By a canyon like a wound gnashed deep through in the granite. A canyon like the maw of a stone dragon.

A strange unexpected rope bridge hangs silently. Sinisterly.

Beckoning adventure—and danger unimaginable.

Enter *Into Shadow Forest* and savor the most spectacular of page-turning epic fantasy novels. Love unique monsters, riveting battles, and fantastic femme fatales? Then read *Into Shadow Forest* now!

Angels Of The Sword

Read Now!

Crossing Of Shadowed Death

Read Now!

The acclaimed master of fantasy Jonathan Evan Hudson once again shines through with his talented story-telling. Time to enter another stunning awe-inspiring world of dangerous demons, magical mayhem, and action-packed adventure.

A simple demon-hunting mission. The young and lonely Dirk yearns for amazing adventure, for gorgeously under-dressed dancer girls among the towering high ferns. Among the even taller pines of the hot and humid Fern Shadow Forest.

Pine needles everywhere. And so fragrant they made the finest of teas.

Sturdy reliable cobble roads of the Divine Empire cut through the whole entire forest. Providing the only safe passage.

Or so Dirk thought ...

Enjoy this sexy, action-packed epic fantasy adventure from the talented Jonathan Evan Hudson. Love to read an enthralling epic fantasy novel full of stunning rip-roaring battles with creative new monsters? Then go read *Crossing of Shadowed Death* now!

A TASTE OF THE ELF GIRL EFFECT

The acclaimed Jonathan Evan Hudson once again weaves an unforgettable tale brimming with spicy page-turning action and fast-burning enemies-to-lovers passion.

Meet the newly knighted Roo Vorshaya. Sworn to protect humanity in the isolated mountain town of Appleharth. Dreams of action-packed adventure and passionate love under a lovely but sinister strawberry-pink sky.

Love re-ignited by a whiff of the familiar peaches and cream scent of his long-lost childhood girlfriend: the notorious elven witch Amber Peaches.

And endangering everything Roo holds dear.

*Love page-turner novels of epic fantasy? Love reading from dusk to dawn? Then go read **The Elf Girl Effect** now!*

CHAPTER 1

ROO

The sky was a strawberry custard for the eyes, and the same color of the lips Roo yearned to kiss.

So what if the clouds behind him were dark and ominous? The wind gusty and chilled more than the perfect shot of vodka. The taste of rain electrified by lightning-to-be ...

The street was as slim as his chances of success.

The cobble as bumpy as the journey ahead.

And this hill — a steep ascent into danger.

Roo even wore a jerkin woven of the finest dragon scale the son of ~~an~~ thee Exiled Exorcist of Most Notable Notoriety could hope to earn as one of the last members of the Vorshaya Clan.

Yup.

The Vorshaya clan. The once very badassed clan nearly wiped out to protect the greatest of the great Oak of Ages, a source of lightful magic and all from ... something, something he'd hunt down and deal with.

Still, if his mother hadn't been doing scholarly stuff far away at the time ... if she hadn't taken him with her ...

Sigh.

He didn't like to think about it much.

But his jerkin was pale blue as the sky ... wasn't today.

But it was one only worn by the best of the best True TriCross Knights. The big, white triple cross on his chest proclaimed it for all to see.

And a chance to pursue his dream to travel the world.

Slay monsters and save people, without any of that bounty hunter nonsense either.

Explores things, places that no one's ever explored before, or okay, more like no one's explored in living memory ...

Or longer.

His jerkin, it even had the snazziest, puffiest shoulder guards of the palest, bluest cold silver, and they were so so perfectly round that a certain Motherly Scholar of Notable Nagging couldn't hope to find a single fault with.

Just like the trusty pouch she made for him.

Shaped like a chubby triple cross, it was strapped to his waist and she magicked it to hold far more than you'd think it could and weigh so much less.

And just like his pouch, his slacks were as blue as the sky ... wasn't ... today.

And ... okay okay.

Anyways, his boots, and girls were obsessed with footwear or else the boot merchants wouldn't cater to girls so utterly much, so anyways, his boots were a snazzy dark blue suede, like the coming night sky should be (but obviously won't be. Pink sky meant severe storm coming.)

And with the coming storm …

There were even spooky tentacles of mist rising from the street, and that only happened when a serious storm was coming through.

But the not so distant rumbles … wasn't only thunder.

So not much time left …

Good thing he wore a pair of sabers and a whip. One saber was of the bluest, sharpest cold silver, and the other, the blackest, sharpest cold steel, a stronger variant of cold iron, and the whip was made of pretty strong scarlet dragon scales, with the dragon magic woven strongly within the whip.

Good for offense and defense, against magical and nonmagical trouble too.

Sort of.

As long as he didn't whip his eye out, like his mother often teased.

Even more important, his trusty arm guards were both cold silver and cold steel forged together. His left arm guard could extend into a shield. The right held a miniature bow with a string of holy blue magic so that, with the right motion flicking motion, it would fire bolts of holy blue light or unholy violet light.

Perfect for a True TriCross Knight.

His heart raced for the coming battle.

For the girl she would soon save.

Since nothing, absolutely *nothing* raced a heart like that elven fragrance, that whiff of the sweetest of peaches and cream only moments ago in this sweet sweltering hot afternoon.

No doubt about it.

The elf girl of his wildest dream come true. Right now. Here in the sexy flesh ...

Amber Peaches: a lust dream come true.

No.

Thee one and **best** lust dream come true.

And the muddy road here was a nice reminder of years ago, back when Peaches and Row got to quipping each other and their quipping got so fierce it broke out into mud wrestling that if, today their reunion broke into mud wrestling, wow, that would be so sexy amazing ...

Sniiiiiiiff.

It smelled ... surprisingly fresh. Earthy forest mud, no, soil fresh.

The lampposts at the street corners ... they were cold iron. The blackest of cold iron and forged like incredibly narrow, but tall, tulips of utter moonless midnight black.

Ah.

The oil lamps on top were those genie-style lamps to be wicked for the evening and wow, did they make the olive oil merchants rich.

But ... it was the genies inside that kept the mud clean. Kept their lamps lit at night, but what those genies were ...

Elf girls captured and lamped into genies due to the war

between humans and demons, and well, elves were demons after all, and elves were the fully evolved form of fairies.

Even Peaches.

But the rumble of distant thunder that wasn't thunder was almost louder than his own tummy rumbling for some peaches and cream pie, especially after that sexy whiff of long missed Peaches.

(All better to tease Peaches with too.)

((Sure, elves should thank the Light their natural body odor, after lots of sweaty work, was so fruity nice rather than so gut-wrenching stinky like humans, you know, like him, but either way, frequenting the public baths, a necessity, human or elf.))

(But not first date material.)

((Outside of certain smut rags kept hidden under the best lock and key in an undisclosed location.))

(((*Very* undisclosed.)))

Even now, the sun was still as blonde as Peaches' waist-long hair, so no worries.

Last they ran into each other, back before war and puberty tore them apart, her hair was ass-long but also far far messier.

Just like back then, she styled the bangs to fountain off the sides of her head like gorgeously floppy wings, plus a floppy witch hat of rosy pink, that, of course, would hide her huuuuge but adorably pointy elf ears.

Ears so long and pointy, that resembled a cross between kitty and fawn ears, especially how they always were moving about so expressively.

So all in all, he wasn't so distracted by her fine ass in a finer minidress, (and it was the ultra-short, ultra snug and stretchy kind that was like strawberry custard to the eyes, ears, and loins,) so no, in that critical moment, he didn't walk into a wall.

No.

He walked into a door.

And as the Light would have it, there was plenty of wall he could of walked into.

The stone floors of the half-timber houses all along this block. All painted as colorfully as a field of wildflowers, but full of apples, apple blossoms, and even more apples.

This town was called Appleharth for a reason.

A very good reason.

And the door he did walk into was the usual solid sturdy oak, so no worries, it took the beating well.

Sure, there was ... a crack down the middle of the door now.

Sure. From him.

But the door's paint job was still spectacular.

No clumsy clod could hope to ruin those artful swathes of banana streaks full of cherry swirls. In fact, there wasn't even a nick to show for his clumsy moment.

Other than a wide crack down the middle.

And by the hinges too.

Roo credited his snazzy cowl and mouth cloth for softening the blow. They were as pale blue as the sky ... wasn't ... today.

But they were the color of Peaches' bright blue eyes ...

well, last time they ran into each other years and years ago, over a decade ago. More than a decade ago. Wait. Same thing. Okay.

Good.

Dazed but not confused. A door would not stop him.

Or delay him.

Much.

Now one more chance or else ... he'd regret it for the rest of his life.

CHAPTER 2
PEACHES

Totally fucking ... that poster of parchment ... those blocky black letters spelling WANTED ...

Oh, for the Oak of Ages ... Peaches totally fucking wanted to give the middle finger to that sly sneak of a trickster the moment she spotted that parchment poster hanging all cozy and sinister and sooo much like a little black widow on those shutters behind the windowsill of those stinkier than stinky roses.

The sky wouldn't be the only one growling soon.

Good thing Peaches wore her finger loop gloves snug and ready. Each was as scarlet red as she'd soon make that trickster, what's her face, the Rouge Reapist, and even better, there were pentacles of unicorn hair woven into each palm to speed up her magic casting faster than a fox pouncing a mouse.

Along the glove were cute heart-shaped gaps. Normally,

they'd hold rosy pink hearts, each of which held a precast spell she could fling at a target for instant effect, but she ran out a while ago and seeing a human alchemist ... pretty dangerous when her kind made such good ingredients to those sorts.

But that thunder close by, not just thunder.

The narrow street echoed the rumble and only confirmed the groan of a dire ogre coming this way.

Strange how there weren't any screams.

Disturbing, in fact.

Regular people shouldn't be so calm around one, unless ... no.

Peaches didn't want to think of it.

Yet.

It was bad enough that the pink sky, as lovely as it was, meant the coming storm would be terrible, if her father's stories held any truth to them.

(Big if.)

But no telling what these half-timber houses were hiding then. So what if they were beautifully decorated with apples, apples, and more apples? Plus a flower or two.

A chill seemed to ache her whole spine.

A warning of danger.

Demonic danger.

Nearby.

Never mind elves were technically lightspawn, a kind of demon, but of the light, so too many humans, sigh.

Least she usually could be reborn a few more times.

More than a few, actually.

Nine lives, like a cat, but three already used, but least her power and beauty were upped each time, but she started out as a brand new fairy, hatching from the Oak of Ages, and had to find another compatible human girl to fuse with, eat her soul and sigh.

No wonder some human despised demons of all sorts.

If her brother only had one life ... if she only had one life ... like these humans ... sigh.

Why Roo even understood way back when ... sigh.

But the lamppost of black iron, horribly styled like tall and narrow tulips, no, that burn to their smell, a burn like that death pepper chili that little brat Roo tricked her stupid bratty self into trying long ago (and stupid her tried it again and again and again ...)

But it was definitely cold iron.

A quick way to a really, really awful death.

No wonder she couldn't pinpoint the source of demonic danger.

No doubt it was darkspawn demons but so what?

This was just a step toward her true dream, becoming an elf witch explorer, and discover why there's so many ruins appearing here and there, and elves had extension records proving some of these ruins appeared without a civilization before, as if it had been moved there.

Some even came from the future.

Others were from the distant past. Ruins that should no longer exist.

Ruins full of monsters.

So today, good practice.

Peaches made a point to keep strutting down the road without hesitation or obvious concern.

If orcs were hunting her ... letting them know she sensed something suspicious, especially as a witch with her fore-sense able to detect danger and ill intent toward her, well, according to her training, a big no no.

And despite it being in the early afternoon, the shutters of all the half-timber houses were shut.

Locked.

Other human towns she'd been in ... plenty of dumb human girls overlooked her demonic side and drooled over her looks, but here, today? Nope. Not one dumbass to brush off.

Something was off.

Good thing she could summon her bow and arrows of light quicker than any other elf in her generation, guy or girl. Several split seconds ahead of the best of the best guys and rapid fire better too. She could even build up plenty of blessed arrows as long as she got enough sunlight during the day, each day to build up and store more blessings for arrows for when she'd need them.

At least if any orc managed to get too close, the stiletto heels of her thigh boots could double as slyly placed daggers.

Alicorn style. Beauty and power came together for elf girls, so lucky her.

And her alicorn was the high grade spiraled kind.

Her boots were as scarlet red as she'd made those orcs.

Normally, she had rosy pink hearts lacing them snug up

her leg. They normally would hold spells she could fling off for instant magical attacks just like her gloves.

But right now, like her gloves, they were just a bunch of heart-shaped gaps.

At least her rosy pink minidress and witch hat were woven with silk of a spellbinder silkworm. They weren't protective against blade and fang, or even against magic ... but they both together were a huge reserve of extra magic that naturally refilled as long as she wore them enough, especially in sunlight.

Even today.

And to fuck with the mind of those perverted orc bastards, she went with the sluttiest minidress she could manage. Translucent silk, so the right angles, the right nude elf deluxe, he-he.

So double the weirdness that no human guys went lusty dumbass toward her today.

Not even the gate guards.

Okay. Gate guards rarely did. Being a guard was all reputation and honor, not about coin. Any act tarnishing that, tarnished all the guards, and the guard loathed that.

Plus, her rosy pink minidress had the perfect distract and destroy notch down the front. One that showed far more than the little it covered.

Including her bra of ruby hearts.

And her chest, buxom to the extreme.

With only a few stretched to the breaking ruby ties down each the notches, the slutty side notches revealed more than just her tasty midriff, they revealed a good solid hint of her lace panties.

Ruby lace.

Orcs were rapeholic monsters, after all. She might as well use their lust smitten idiocy against them.

Roo would so laugh and approve.

(And leer.)

((Leer plenty.))

(((Sigh. *Boys.*)))

((((But if he didn't ... her pointy tipped boots, his rear, he-he.))))

WANT MORE?

Go to

WANT MORE?

Go to

www.JonathanEvanHudson.com